THE RANCHER AND THE *Lady*

THE ROYAL AGENTS OF MI6

BOOK FOUR

USA TODAY BESTSELLING AUTHOR

HEATHER SLADE

THE RANCHER AND THE LADY
© 2021 Heather Slade

Paperback:
978-1-953626-40-0

MORE FROM AUTHOR HEATHER SLADE

Table of Contents

Prologue

Quint

January

I stretched my arms above my head and looked out at the sunrise. Typically, I'd be out, riding the ranch by now, but today, my crew was handling the morning chores on their own.

Before coming in last night, I'd asked my men to cover for me. I hadn't needed to explain why; they all knew the mahogany-haired beauty asleep next to me was on the ranch and had been for the last three days.

They spared me the jabs they would've shared with one another under the same circumstances, perhaps sensing the woman was more than a warm body to keep me company on a cold night.

In her sleep, she'd kicked off the blankets and sheet, so her luscious body was on full display, illuminated by the bronze, orange, and yellow hues of the sun's rays streaming in through the window.

The last time she came to visit, she stayed three months but only spent half of that time in my bed.

Later this morning, she'd be leaving, and I wasn't sure she'd ever be back.

Deep inside, part of me wanted to ask her to stay, but we both knew I never would. If Darrow Whittaker ever decided she wanted more than a few laughs coupled with the best sex I'd ever had in my life, she knew where to find me. I couldn't promise I'd be sitting around, waiting on her, though.

"I thought we were sleeping in," she groaned in her sexier-than-shit English accent. When she covered her eyes with her forearm, I couldn't help but lean over and lave the nipple that was now pointed directly at me.

"God, Quint." Darrow's groan turned into a moan as she held my head to her breast.

"Are you sore, baby?" I asked, moving one hand lower.

She shook her head.

"Not good enough. Let me hear the words."

This time, instead of a groan or moan, Darrow growled. When I laughed, she smacked my arm, which only made me laugh harder.

She pushed me until I was on my back and nipped at my neck before trailing her lips down my body.

"Shadow," I said in my most menacing tone.

"I'm leaving today, Quint. If I'm sore, I'll recover."

I pulled her up the front of my body so her chin rested on my sternum. "Let's shower."

"Showering means getting out of bed."

I rolled so she was under me, and then stood. "My understanding was that you had an early flight."

She stuck out her lower lip in a pout. "I do, which is why I don't want to waste time now."

"I like the idea of leaving you wanting more," I said, walking from the bed into the en suite bathroom.

— Darrow —

Instead of following, I lay in bed listening to the sound of water turning on and the shower door closing behind him.

Why had I agreed to leave with Doc and Merrigan today? Because if I hadn't, I'd be flying back to England rather than just out to California. At least, by continuing my training on the Central Coast, there was a possibility Quint might come to visit me.

I knew he wouldn't, but still, there was a better chance he'd take a two-hour flight over a ten-hour one.

My eyes opened wide when I heard him come into the bedroom; I must've drifted off. I turned and studied the man walking toward me.

His bronze skin was taut over his magnificently contoured arm muscles, and he smelled like the outdoors, even now when he'd just gotten out of the shower. His stomach was ripped in a classic six-pack, tapering to a perfect "V." When he turned around to get something from his wardrobe, I feasted my eyes on his back that was as toned as his front. The rippling muscles of his thighs and his rock-hard arse left me breathless.

He turned back to face me after putting on his jeans—not trousers, he'd told me. A tangle of dark hair peeked out of his bulging fly.

"Are you sure there isn't anything I can do for you, cowboy?"

"You know I can't get enough of you, Shadow," he said, using the nickname a second time that I'd grown to love and had missed hearing so much. Quint let the jeans slide off those well-muscled thighs until he was, again, gloriously naked.

I licked my lips.

"Like what you see, darlin'?" he teased in his Texan drawl, his voice so deep that the vibrations of it heated my core. His searing gaze met mine, and I held my hand out to him.

"Ask me to stay," I whispered.

Instead of saying the words I longed to hear, Quint kissed the back of my hand before sliding in next to me. I rested my head on his chest and he wrapped me in his arms.

"This is a great opportunity for you, Shadow. I remember hearing stories about Burns Butler and Leech Hess from Deck and my pa."

I smiled at his use of "pa" over "father."

Anyone who'd met Archer "Z" Alexander knew he was about as far from a "pa" as a man could get. The ranch had been his home base for many years before his wife, Quint's mother, passed away, but he'd still traveled endlessly on behalf of his job with the Security Service, also known as MI5. He'd eventually risen through the ranks of the United Kingdom's domestic counterintelligence and security agency and was named director general. Last year, Z had been pro-moted to chief of MI6, the international Secret Intelligence Service branch.

Like me, Quint had grown up surrounded by people in the intelligence community. The difference between them, though, was I always felt like an outsider amongst a group of people I longed desperately to be on the inside with.

Quint, on the other hand, was perfectly comfortable living his life as a cowboy on his family's hundred-thousand-acre ranch.

There'd been a time I was just as comfortable here—until the man who was like a second father to me fell gravely ill and I was called back to England.

That was the cog that had set the whole train in motion in terms of my life and what I wanted to do with it.

Maybe if I hadn't been offered the slot at Fort Monckton, MI6's training center, I would've been content here still. But the idea that the dreams I'd had since I was a little girl were within my reach, was something I couldn't ignore. I made my choice, just like Z once had, to serve Her Majesty, the Queen.

Quint squeezed my shoulder. "Earth to Darrow."

"What? Sorry. Got lost in thought for a moment. Yes, you're right. It is quite the opportunity."

His voice grew softer. "Go out and grab your dreams, Shadow. Don't tell me to ask you to stay."

"I don't know when I'll ever be back," I said, my eyes filling with tears.

"So be it, darlin'."

"That's it? What will be, will be?"

Quint took his arm from around me and turned his body so we were facing each other. "I've made my decisions, Darrow. I know what kind of life I want and where I want to live it. No one can make that decision for another person. You've figured out what you want, and it isn't waking up before dawn to traipse out to a barn and feed cattle. I respect that in the same way I expect you to respect my choices."

"What if we never see one another again?" I wished I'd see some kind of emotion play out on Quint's face, but none did.

"Like I said, Darrow. So be it."

Part 1

1

Quint

Previous August

"Hey, Pa," I said, answering my father's call and knowing the first thing he'd do would be to laugh.

"Hello, son. I wish there were some equally cow-poke-type phrase I could greet you with."

"Boy. That works."

My father, known to most—including me—as Z, laughed again.

"Not that I don't love talking to you, but to what do I owe the honor of this particular call?"

"How's your sister?"

I sighed. Seven months ago, Wren had shown up back on the ranch saying she was taking a leave of absence from her job with the NGA—the National Geospatial-Intelligence Agency—a branch of the United State's National Security Agency.

She hadn't offered up any details, and I hadn't asked. I sensed there was more to it than a simple leave of absence, but I had no idea what.

"She puts one foot in front of the other," I finally said.

"I was afraid of that."

Wren rode out with me every day, helping with whatever chores needed to be done, just like she had as a teenager. However, there was no light in her green eyes.

"I have a favor to ask," said my father.

"Shoot."

"You are familiar with the Whittaker family?"

"Not really."

"There's a daughter who finds herself a bit out of sorts. She came to me looking for your sister, actually."

"And?" I could guess where this conversation was headed, but I'd rather have Z spell it out for me.

"I'd like to offer Darrow respite on the ranch for a time."

"How long?"

"Open-ended."

"You said you were asking a favor, but this ranch is as much yours as it is mine."

"I don't live there, Quint. You do. And for the time being, so does your sister. I don't want to inundate or inconvenience you."

I chuckled. "With over a hundred thousand acres, I think I'll be able to find somewhere to disappear for a while if the added estrogen overwhelms me."

"Thank you, Quint."

"No need to thank me, Pa, but I appreciate the heads-up. When is she due to arrive?"

"Two days from now, and I'll be escorting her. There's one more thing, Quint. I'd like to keep this visit a surprise for Wren."

I laughed out loud. "You mean to say, you don't want her to know this woman is on the way."

"Your sister was…involved with one of Darrow's older brothers."

That explained a great deal although, like before, I had no intention of asking Wren about it. "She doesn't like secrets, Z."

"That's why I'm coming with Darrow. Now that I'm assured you have no issues with the visit, you can forget this conversation took place."

"Roger that," I answered, shaking my head and smiling. "See you soon, Pa."

I could hear my father's laughter as I ended the call.

I walked over and looked out the kitchen window. I loved my simple life here on the ranch, free from the drama that had led my sister, and now this other woman, here.

Sure, it got lonely from time to time, and was maybe a little too remote, but a night in either Austin or San Antonio usually assuaged my yearning for companionship enough that I couldn't wait to get back home.

This time of year, though, there was no reason to visit the big city. The ranch's manager, Decker, three other hands, and myself competed in ranch rodeos all over the region.

Every weekend there were several team roping events to choose from. Since we weren't in it for the money, we always picked the ranch rodeos over any other. It was more about the competition and the fun we had after the day's events were over and the participants and spectators stayed to play.

"Good morning, Quint," said Wren, joining me in the kitchen. "Who were you talking to?"

"Z."

Wren didn't ask why our father had called. Instead, she walked over and poured herself a cup of coffee.

"What's on the board today?" she asked, standing next to me as I looked out at our land.

"Movin' cattle out to the southwest pastures."

"Good," she answered, washing her cup.

"You should eat somethin' before you head out."

My sister nodded and walked out of the house. It wasn't different than any other day since she'd shown up on the ranch. She looked like she'd dropped twenty pounds, on a frame that didn't have that much to lose. I could encourage her to eat more, but she was a grown-ass woman; it wasn't up to me to make sure she didn't waste away to nothing. She was my little sister, though, and I couldn't help but look out for her.

Instead of making my usual two-sandwich lunch, I made three, threw them in my day pack, and walked out of the house like she had.

It was hotter than hell this time of year in Texas. I was already sweating and I hadn't gotten all the way back to the barn after my morning break. I wiped my brow with a handkerchief and approached the stall where my horse, Gunsmoke, stood at the ready.

This morning I'd taken PeeWee out just to get the giant of a horse some exercise before it got too hot.

The fifteen-hundred-pound American quarter horse stood at almost sixteen hands and was approaching his thirtieth birthday. I figured the big old boy had at least five good years left in him, but that didn't mean I'd push him, especially in this heat.

My Paint, Gunsmoke, on the other hand, was a fifteen-hand, six-year-old gelding. The horse was happiest out, working the land and could go all day. I doubted he was over a thousand pounds, and if he was, it was all muscle. There were five other horses in the string I rode day-in, day-out throughout the year, but there was no question that Gunsmoke was my favorite.

"C'mon, boy." As I led the horse out of the stall, something caught my eye. I tied off Gunsmoke and walked over to take a look.

Wren's back was to me, and her cheek rested against her horse, Spark. I could tell by the rise and fall of her shoulders that she was crying. Instead of confronting her, I backed away, walked over to Gunsmoke, and led him out of the barn.

I hoped our father knew what he was doing, allowing this woman to visit the ranch. My sister was private; I'd be surprised if she felt comfortable confiding in a woman whose brother was the likely reason for her tears.

2

Darrow

I looked out the window of the plane at what looked like scorched earth. Texas was so different from Bedfordshire, the setting of the dukedom that had been in my family for generations. But this is what I'd wanted—a total departure from life as I knew it.

Sighing, I rolled my shoulders in an attempt to shrug away the anxiety that settled in them whenever I thought about "home."

"I appreciate this, Z," I said for the innumerable time when the pilot announced we were getting ready to land.

"Wren will be happy to see you."

"Not as happy as I'll be to see her."

Wren was the first person in my life who worked in intelligence and didn't talk to me like I wouldn't be capable of following along or understanding. While I hadn't seen her since January, I hoped our friendship would continue to be as easy as it was the day we met, back when my brother Sutton was still with MI5 and he brought the mysterious agent to the abbey for the first time.

***

"Yes, Thornton," I answered when my oldest brother, the current duke, called. We'd had a spat the day before, and I was in no mood to listen to him scold me a second time.

Thornton cleared his throat. "I called for two reasons. The first is to apologize for yesterday. I was out of line."

If he expected me to apologize too, he would be sorely disappointed. He'd been lecturing me about taking on a more active social schedule with some of the charities our mother, the former duchess and now dowager, supported.

I'd tried to explain that wasn't the life I wanted to lead, which only led to Thornton lecturing me about duty to service. I understood that part of it, I just couldn't make him see that I wanted to serve in an entirely different way.

"What was the second reason for your call?"

"I wanted you to know that Sutton has a visitor on premises."

"In what way is that relevant?"

"A female visitor."

I laughed. My brothers were both such unbelievable gossips. "Thanks for letting me know. Was there anything else?"

He sighed. "Darrow, please let's not carry this any further. I told you I was sorry. Please forgive me."

Since he had only asked for my forgiveness rather than an apology in return, I would be gracious. "I do forgive you, Thornton, and thank you, sincerely."

No sooner had I ended that call than my mobile rang again.

"Hello, Sutton," I said when I saw his name pop up on the screen. "I heard you're out roaming the estate with an attractive woman."

"Wondering if she might be able to borrow something to ride in."

"Yes, of course, if you think…" I was about to say something ridiculous like "if we wear the same size," but that was one of Sutton's superpowers, it seemed.

He told me they'd be there shortly and rang off.

When I opened the door and invited Sutton and his friend in, I saw my brother hadn't been far off in his assumption that she and I were the same size.

"Wren, I'd like you to meet my sister, Darrow, duchess-in-training and all-around imp. Darrow, this is Wren."

I visibly bristled at my brother's duchess comment and hoped that Wren didn't think my annoyance had anything to do with her. It was just that after my spat with Thornton yesterday on the subject, the last thing I intended to endure was more of the same from Sutton.

"Come with me," I said to Wren, motioning for her to follow when my brother excused himself to the lavatory.

"I really appreciate this," she said with an accent I didn't expect. "I hope it's not too much of a bother."

"It isn't any bother at all," I told her, pulling trousers and jumpers from my wardrobe. "I keep my riding boots at the barn, but it looks as though you and I wear the same size, so you should be fine."

"Again, thank you."

When I asked where she was from, Wren's cheeks turned pink.

She laughed. "Texas."

"Is that funny?"

Wren shook her head. "Your brother. When we met yesterday, he said I was pretty as a Georgia peach, but in an accent that sounded like a cross between…" Wren laughed again. "I don't even know how to describe it other than I don't think there's a state in the union that would've claimed that affected accent as their own."

"He's a right wanker sometimes. I hope you gave it right back to him."

"Rest assured, I did. Then, and at dinner."

Clearly, Wren found whatever had transpired between her and my brother in the last twenty-four hours highly amusing. Which, of course, made me laugh too.

"I hope you made him take you somewhere posh."

"Five Hertford, although not at my suggestion."

I raised a brow. "The poshest. Well done, Wren. I think we're going to get on quite well."

"You know," she said, putting a hand on her hip. "I think we are too. I feel as though we've met before. Does that sound crazy?"

"Not at all, actually." I looked at the clothes laid out on my bed. "I'll let you try these on if you'd like. I'll wait downstairs and tease my brother endlessly."

"She's lovely," I said to my brother with a wink.

"Stop it."

"What? You do realize that this is the first time you've brought a woman to the abbey since you were in upper school."

"Don't be ridiculous, and please lower your voice."

"It's true. I see why, though. She's...nice. Not exactly who I might've expected, but better."

When Wren appeared at the top of the stairs, I watched my brother's face light up like I'd never seen before. Had he finally met his proverbial match? I hoped so. Wren was lovely, as I'd said to him, and seemed like great fun.

***

"Miss, please return your seat back to its upright position," the flight attendant said, touching my arm.

"Oh, sorry. I was lost in thought."

The woman walked away without acknowledging I'd spoken. How rudely American of her.

"Well, that won't do," I mumbled, shaking my head.

"What's that? What won't do?" asked Z.

"I was silently disparaging the manners of the country that I hope to make my permanent home."

Z both laughed and raised a brow. "Ranch life is different than what you're accustomed to, Darrow."

"Which is precisely what I'm looking for. A fresh start, a new life, in a place as different from Whittaker Abbey as possible."

Z didn't respond, and I was grateful for it. I knew that he, like my brothers, expected me to fit in the mold of an English noblewoman—a role that couldn't be further from the way I saw myself.

3

Quint

I looked up at the same time Wren did and watched the SUV as it was engulfed by a cloud of dust spun up from its barreling over the gravel road toward the main house.

"Who's that?" she asked.

"Somebody to see you."

"Who?"

"Darrow Whittaker. Said she's a friend of yours from England."

"What's she want?"

I shook my head, wishing I weren't in the middle of this. "What do friends usually want?" Instead of sticking around to answer more questions, I rode off in the opposite direction.

A short while later, I saw my father on horseback, riding toward me.

"How pissed is she?" I asked when he approached.

"Hard to tell. I think after the shock of how long Darrow plans to stay wore off, she remembered her manners along with how much she liked Wilder's sister."

"Wilder?" Was that someone's name?

"I told you Wren was involved with one of Darrow's brothers. Sutton Whittaker is his name. He's currently interim chief of MI6."

"How long did she tell Wren she planned to stay?"

"If she had her way, she'd never leave."

Only a couple of days ago, I'd told Z that this ranch belonged to the three of us. I couldn't very well change my mind now and question who came to visit or for what length.

"How long are you staying?" I asked him.

"Not long. Just until I'm certain Darrow is comfortable here."

"Better make sure Tee-Tee knows we'll have two more for dinner," I suggested.

"I took care of it."

"How about a beer, then? I could use one myself."

"Sounds good, boy," answered Z with a wink.

"What's she runnin' away from?" I asked on our ride back to the house.

"The same thing your sister is."

"Is this woman's life in danger?"

Z shook his head. "No, a failed relationship, I fear."

"What do they think this is, a dude ranch?"

"Yes," said my father, nodding. "I'm certain that's exactly the way your sister sees King-Alexander Ranch."

Z rode ahead, and I didn't care. I didn't really mean Wren, even though her inclusion was assumed when I used the word "they" instead of "she."

By the time I got back to the barn, my father was already in the house—exactly the way I'd planned it. The only thing I felt bad about was that Tee-Tee and Wren were probably holding dinner until I got inside, and that wasn't fair to anyone.

One of the ranch hands offered to take Gunsmoke. Under normal circumstances, I'd take care of my horse myself, but in this case, I didn't want to delay dinner any longer. Not to mention that my mama would be turning in her grave if she knew how poorly I was treating a guest upon her arrival at the ranch that had been in the King family for generations.

I hurried and washed up, went through the back door of the house so I could change out of my work clothes, and rushed down the hallway toward the dining room where I could hear my father and sister speaking to our guest.

I hesitated and listened. Darrow Whittaker's voice was like that of an angel. I'd always thought that girls from my home state had the most beautiful voices, but the soft-spoken woman with the English lilt had them beat by a Texas mile.

I was about to take another step when she laughed. *Damn.* If this woman was half as pretty as she sounded—wait—I couldn't think about that. She was a guest in our home for an indefinite amount of time. Plus, she was here because some Englishman broke her sweet little heart.

I stopped in the kitchen to apologize to Tee-Tee for holding up dinner before joining the others in the dining room. She just shook her head and smiled like she usually did. Working on a ranch for all the years she had, she knew there was rarely a set time for any meal.

"There he is," said my father when I joined them. "Come and meet our guest."

I looked beyond Z to where the most beautiful creature I'd ever seen stood talking and laughing with my sister. Half as pretty as she sounded? Hell, she was twice as pretty.

The ends of her long dark hair, even tied up in a ponytail, brushed the curve of her spine. I recognized the pink tank top and short denim skirt she wore, as well as her sandals—they belonged to Wren. However, they'd never looked half as good on her.

She turned and faced me when I approached.

"Welcome to King-Alexander Ranch," I said, taking her outstretched hand in mine. "I'm Quint."

"It's a pleasure to meet you, Quint, and thank you for your hospitality. I'm Darrow Whittaker."

When she shook my hand, I didn't want to let go. Instead of one of those limp-wristers, Darrow's grip was strong. And those dark-brown eyes—damn—they looked right into my soul.

"How about dinner?" said Wren, clearing her throat.

I dropped Darrow's hand and motioned for the two women to go ahead of me.

"Don't…even…think…about it," Wren seethed through gritted teeth when her friend was just out of earshot.

I held both hands up in surrender and laughed, but Wren didn't.

"I mean it, Quint. Let her be."

"I heard ya, sis."

Z lagged behind, so I did too.

"I'm leaving in the morning, unless you have a particular reason for me to stay."

"Nah. Life ain't gonna be much different for me, Pa."

"Your dear mother would box my ears, hearing you talk that way," he groaned.

"We'll be fine, Z. Go home."

"I'll have a chat with Wren when we're finished."

I nodded. As soon as dinner was over, I planned to hightail it outta here. In fact, as long as Miss Darrow Whittaker was a guest at King-Alexander Ranch, I planned to make myself scarce. It was the only way I could ensure that I'd keep my hands to myself like my sister had warned me to.

Tee-Tee had made chicken enchiladas with beans and rice for our guest, and there was a pitcher of what I guessed were frozen margaritas on the sideboard.

"Can I pour a glass for anyone?" I asked when I got one for myself.

"I'd love one," said Darrow. "What is it?"

I almost looked up at the ceiling. Beautiful, obviously a great sense of humor, and adventurous. Maybe I should consider going to England with Z because the woman smiling at me from the other side of the room was all sorts of everything I liked.

Wren answered Darrow when I didn't, telling her all about Tee-Tee's frozen concoction.

"She won't tell anyone what the secret ingredient is," said Wren.

"I know what it is," I said, setting Darrow's drink on the table.

"You do not." Wren stood to get herself a glass.

"I would've gotten it for you," I muttered.

"Sit down and eat, Quint," Wren said over her shoulder. "And don't lie. I know damn well Tee-Tee would never tell you."

"Ever consider the possibility that I got some of Z's spy blood in me? You're not the only spook in this house, you know."

Wren spun around and looked at Darrow. *Shit.* She didn't know? How the hell was that possible?

"It's okay," the beguiling creature said, resting her hand on my forearm. "Both my brothers are with SIS.

Or they were. I know more than most people think I do. We're probably the same that way."

I looked from Darrow's hand up to her eyes. Was this woman even real? The warmth that was traveling up my arm from her touch sure felt real.

"Excuse me." I got up from the table. "Anyone need hot sauce?" I was halfway to the kitchen when I heard Z say there was already some on the table, but I kept walking.

"You don't know my secret ingredient," muttered Tee-Tee when I went into the kitchen. "You're just showing off for the pretty *senorita*."

"You found me out," I said to the woman who had been the head cook at the ranch for as long as I could remember. What Wren and I would've done without her after our mother died, I didn't know.

I put my arm around the tiny woman, leaned over, and kissed her temple. "I gotta get back out to the barn, but save me some of that delicious dinner, will you?"

She shook her head and handed me a foil-covered plate.

"Who's this for?"

"You, *mijo*. I'll let them know you were called away."

"Thanks, Tee-Tee. I love ya."

4

Darrow

There was no doubt my cheeks were bright red. It's what always happened when I was embarrassed. What had caused Wren's brother to get up so abruptly and not just leave the table but, according to the woman Wren had called Tee-Tee, leave the house entirely?

"Mister Quint was called away," the woman reported. "He apologizes."

Had I been too forward when I put my hand on his arm? And if so, was that reason to walk away from the dinner table? I was merely trying to be friendly.

No matter. I'd overstepped, and I'd be sure not to make that mistake again. The cowboy was likely disgruntled about my being here at all. Maybe he, like most people in my life, believed I was a spoiled "duchess-in-training" as my brother Sutton had called me. I wasn't, and I'd prove it to him. I'd spent much of my childhood at the knee of Whittaker Abbey's head groundskeeper, Wellie. I knew all about hard work.

I tried to stifle a yawn and put my hand over my mouth, discreetly looking at the time when I did. It was two in the morning in England, and after a long day of traveling, I was exhausted. Plus, I intended to hit the ground running tomorrow and prove I wasn't merely a houseguest to be entertained. If I had my way, I'd never return to England again, except to visit. If I was going to make that dream come true, I had to create a life for myself here. Perhaps once I got my footing at King-Alexander Ranch, I could go work at some other Texas ranch.

Duchess-in-training? Hell, no. That wasn't the life I'd ever wanted, and since the kind I'd always dreamed of was too far out of reach, this one would do instead.

"You must be exhausted," said Wren.

"I am. I'm so sorry to be a spoilsport on my first night here."

"Not at all. Come with me."

I stood when Wren did, and picked up my plate.

"Leave that," she said. "Tee-Tee will take care of it."

"Please let me help. I don't want anyone to think I came here on holiday." *Especially your brother,* I wanted to add.

"I'll tell you what. Tomorrow we'll ride out, and you can get a taste for ranch life. Tonight, get some rest."

"Days on the ranch start early, Darrow," said Z. "When Wren says you'll ride out, she means at sunrise."

"That isn't necessary, Z. Let the poor woman get acclimated to the time at least. Just because Quint's day begins that early doesn't mean mine always does."

"What time is dawn?" I asked.

"Five," answered Wren, glaring at her father.

"Not a problem. That's eleven London time." I winked at Z and followed Wren out of the room.

"Don't listen to him. You're a guest here."

When Wren stopped in the hallway, I did too. I put my hand on her forearm like I'd done with Quint, glad that she didn't react the way her brother had. "I meant what I said. I'm not on holiday, Wren. At least I don't want to be."

She sighed and looked into my eyes. "I'm sorry about you and Axel."

I shrugged. "Don't be. That's over, and I'm ready to start the next chapter of my life."

It looked as though Wren wanted to say something more, but when she didn't, I said good night.

"Where are you going?" she asked when I continued down the hallway.

"Z said that your brother told him to put my trunk in here. Did you mean for me to have a different room?"

"No, it's fine. If that's where Quint told him. It's best, really. We won't disturb you in the morning."

She looked puzzled, but I was too tired to continue questioning her tonight. If I was in the wrong room, I'd switch tomorrow and offer to change the bedding.

"If you need anything, let me know." Wren hesitated before turning to leave. "I'm really glad you're here, Darrow."

It was still dark outside when my eyes sprung open. I checked the time; it was a little after four, which meant I'd slept for almost eight hours.

I rolled out of bed and grabbed riding clothes from my trunk. At least I'd been smart enough to pack those, knowing I was headed to a ranch. They may not be the perfect attire for the work I intended to do today, but they'd do. Maybe I could talk Wren into taking me shopping later today or tomorrow—after the chores were done, of course.

Knowing it would likely be as hot or hotter later than it was yesterday, I plaited my long, wet hair after I finished showering and then crept into the kitchen, hoping I could find a kettle and tea bags before anyone else was up.

"Bloody hell," I said under my breath, seeing Quint had beat me into the kitchen.

"Good morning," he said before I had a chance to retreat back to the bedroom.

"Good morning."

"You're up mighty early," he commented, taking a cup out of the cupboard. "Coffee?"

"As I told Wren last night, it's almost noon London time."

"Sleep well?" he asked.

"Very, thank you."

"How do you take it?" He poured me a cup of the dark brew.

I was about to ask if he had tea, but thought better of it. "A little cream, please? If you have it."

"Is that a question?"

"No. Not a question."

Quint grinned and took a glass bottle out of the refrigerator. "Fresh from the cow," he said, setting it on the counter near me. "Ever milked a cow, Darrow?"

"Can't say I have. However, I do know how to muck a stall."

Quint turned just in time to see me cringe after my first taste of coffee.

"Need some sugar, darlin'?" He reached for the door of another cupboard.

"No, thank you."

"You sure?"

He was laughing at me, at least with his eyes, and I didn't like it.

"When do we ride out?" I asked rather than respond a second time. I knew my own bloody mind and didn't like sugar in my tea either.

"About to head out there now myself. You'll do best to wait for my sister."

"I'm prepared to go with you."

He looked down at my riding boots. "Not in those, you aren't."

I traipsed down the hall to the bedroom and grabbed my Wellies. "Better?" I asked when I came back into the kitchen.

He half smiled. "All right, then. Let's get out there. By the way, tea's right here." He opened yet another cupboard and pointed to a cannister.

"I'm fine with coffee, thank you."

If he made coffee in the morning, that's what I'd drink, and I'd learn to like it. I wanted no special treatment, and that included my morning beverage.

"This here's the board," he said, pointing to the obvious when we got to the barn. "If you're first out, check this, and you'll know what to get started on."

"When do you milk the cows?"

"I don't. No one does. There are machines for that."

"Ever milked a cow, Mr. Alexander?"

He smiled. "Sure as sugar have, sugar. And we do away with formality around these parts. I answer to Quint."

"Mornin', Fish," said a man who walked up behind me. "Who's this?"

"This is Darrow Whittaker," Quint answered. "Visiting from England. Darrow, this is Decker. He's the ranch manager. Aren't many days when someone beats ol' Deck to the barn. You draggin' today, buddy?"

"Nice to meet you, ma'am," Decker said, and then rubbed the back of his neck. "Missed ya up at the Branch last night, Fish."

Quint eyed the man, and they both grinned. I assumed "Fish" was an inside joke. I didn't mind being excluded; it had been that way most of my life. If they thought a little cowboy humor first thing in the morning would rattle me, they should try accidentally walking in on a hot wash after a mission in which several people were killed.

"Miss Whittaker here is going to ride out with us today, Deck. Who you want her to mount?"

The look passed between them again, but the meaning of that particular joke wasn't lost on me.

"Please, do away with the formality, Fish. I answer to Darrow."

Quint laughed out loud. "Follow me," he said, walking me over to a stall. "This is Wren's horse, Spark."

I put my hand on the horse's neck. "Good morning, Spark."

"I'll have you ride Tink today. See how you do. Deck will get her saddled up."

"I can do it. I'm assuming that's the tack room." I pointed to an open door.

"Sure enough," said Quint, leading me over to it.

I went ahead of him and grabbed the tack from the peg with the horse's name above it. "Anything in particular I need to know about her?"

"You're out here early," Wren said, approaching before Quint could respond to my question. "What's up?"

I watched the look that passed between brother and sister. It was an entirely different interaction than the one I'd witnessed moments before with the manager. Wren's hand was on her hip, and Quint looked sheepish.

"Thought I'd get Darrow acquainted with the workings of the ranch," he answered.

"You're so full of shit," Wren muttered, taking Tink's tack out of my hand. "And you're an asshole." Wren stalked past them and hung it back on the peg before grabbing what was below the name Sage.

When she returned, Wren glared at her brother, whose eyebrows were raised. "She can probably outride every one of us," she said to him before turning to me. "You'd be lucky to get out of the nearest pasture on Tink. She doesn't exactly like to get out and work. Sage, on the other hand, you'll enjoy."

We'd been riding for a little over two hours and, so far, hadn't done anything other than explore. I'd paid close attention, though, as Wren explained how the pastures were laid out and the easiest way to identify each of them. Most had some kind of landmark that signified their name.

"We refer to this pasture as Schoolhouse," Wren said, pointing to a dilapidated building that looked like it could've once housed a schoolroom. "Time for breakfast," she added, motioning in the direction of the barns.

"It's so beautiful here, Wren," I said when we slowed the horses to a walk.

"I forget how much so when I'm gone."

I wondered if I'd feel the same when I set foot back on the grounds of Whittaker Abbey.

We let the horses loose in the corral and walked over to the ranch house. "Quint will eat with Deck and the guys down at the bunkhouse this morning," Wren said when we went inside.

"Does he usually?"

"No, not usually. It depends on the time of year, really. I'm sure he's just giving us time on our own."

After being on our own since we rode out? More likely he was avoiding me.

Maybe this hadn't been such a good idea after all. I hadn't considered Wren wasn't the only one who lived here when I'd begged Z to bring me to the ranch. Maybe I was more selfish and inconsiderate than I was trying to convince everyone I was.

"You can tell me if I'm being intrusive, Wren. I know I blindsided you and your brother by just show-ing up here. He didn't even have a say in it."

"Of course he did," said Z, walking up from the back of the house. "I cleared it with him earlier in the week."

"I knew it," Wren mumbled.

"Oh, dear," I muttered.

Z put his arm around my shoulders. "Stop worrying so much. You're welcome here. Isn't that right, Wren?"

"Absolutely." Wren opened the refrigerator and pulled out eggs and bacon. "Hungry, Z?"

He looked at his watch. "I guess I have time to eat before I leave."

"Leave?" I asked. "You're leaving already?"

"Her Majesty's work never ends," he said with a wink.

"We'll take you to the airport. That way we can stop and pick up some cooler clothes for you," Wren said, looking over her shoulder at me.

"Maybe I should just go back with Z."

"Givin' in already?" asked Quint, startling me.

"I thought you and Deck were having breakfast with the crew," said Wren.

"We came up to say goodbye to Z. Heard you say you're taking him to the airport. While you're out, get her a decent pair of work boots." He motioned at me with his thumb and then turned to look me in the eye. "If you're stickin' around, that is."

I met his gaze and squared my shoulders. "I am." I couldn't tell by the look on his face if he was happy or otherwise, but he hardly would've suggested his sister take me to get a pair of work boots if he wanted me to leave, would he?

"Go sit. I can do this," said Wren.

"I'd really like to help. Please."

Wren nodded, and I washed my hands.

Quint, Deck, and Z were sitting at the kitchen's bar, none saying much. I couldn't stand the lack of conversation.

"Why do you call him Fish?" I asked Decker.

"Long story," Quint answered before Deck could.

I waited for either of them to elaborate, but neither did. We spent the next fifteen minutes in relative silence.

"Thanks for breakfast," Quint said five minutes after we began eating. "I gotta get back to work." He stood, and so did Decker and Z. "See you next time, Pa."

"I'll be back soon, boy."

I watched as the two men smiled and embraced, obviously sharing yet another inside joke.

"See ya," Quint muttered as he and Decker walked past Wren and me, and then out the door before I had the chance to respond.

"I don't think he likes me," I murmured.

"Maybe he likes you too much."

"Don't start, Z," admonished Wren. "Let's go, or you'll miss your flight."

5

Quint

I watched the two women get in the SUV with my father, and let out a deep sigh.

"She's a looker," said Decker.

"Yep," I said, chewing on a piece of straw.

"You oughta invite her down to the Branch tonight."

"I don't think so." I walked out to the corral and whistled for Gunsmoke. "I'll be up at Schoolhouse, checking on water, if you need me."

Decker nodded with scrunched eyes.

I was partway up the ridge when I saw the SUV pull out of the ranch gates. Funny how I couldn't wait to see it driving back in.

There'd be no way I'd invite the sweet Miss Darrow to the bar Decker affectionately referred to as the Branch. Not that she wouldn't have fun. No, I had an entirely different reason for not wanting to—once the other cowboys took one look at her, there'd be a line out the door of men waiting to take her time.

"Hold up," I heard Deck say from behind me. "We goin' over to Big Bend on Friday?"

"Why wouldn't we be?"

"You seem preoccupied is all."

"Of course we're goin' to Big Bend. Knock this shit off, Deck."

Between the beginning of June and the end of September, there was a rodeo just about every weekend put on by the WRCA—the Working Ranch Cowboys Association. It was the purest form of rodeo, stemming back to how it all began. One cowboy, or a group of them, from one ranch would brag to another, and pretty soon they'd be circling the trucks and setting up a competition.

Nowadays, the teams were made up of men and women who worked ranches full-time, every day of their lives. The events included bronc riding, team roping, branding, doctoring, and penning, and everyone's favorite, wild-cow milking.

Competing groups were typically sponsored by ranches, just like Decker, me, and the other three members of our team were sponsored by King-Alexander.

Like the better-known, flashier, and in my opinion, less authentic rodeos, the WRCA had a World

Championship event at the beginning of November. We'd gone every year for the last ten, and it was something I looked forward to, whether we won, placed, or none of the above.

"Nothing's changed, Deck, and nothing's going to."

My friend turned and rode away, leaving me feeling as though Deck didn't believe me any more than I did myself. Change was coming; I could feel it. That didn't necessarily mean it was related to the lovely Darrow. It could be anything. There was no denying, though, that it was in the wind.

Hours later, the sun had set on my day, but Wren and Darrow still hadn't gotten back. I'd thought about calling, but I never checked in with her. Doing so now would be completely out of character, which would make Wren suspicious.

I sat on the porch of the ranch house and enjoyed the peacefulness of the night. It was still eighty degrees, but that beat over one hundred, so I wouldn't complain.

As I took another swig from my bottle of beer, I saw the SUV approaching the gate and breathed easier. I thought about getting up and going inside so they didn't think I was waiting for them, but I spent plenty of nights sitting just like I was now. There was no reason for me to feel uncomfortable about it.

I could hear Darrow's laughter as the two women climbed out of the vehicle, and it warmed my heart, not just because the Englishwoman's laugh was so sweet, but also because I hadn't heard my sister laugh so much since we were kids. If nothing else, Z's bringing Darrow here was good for Wren.

"Have fun?" I asked when they approached.

Darrow startled; I could see it from where I sat.

"We had a great time," answered Wren. "Why are you home? I thought you'd be up at the Long Branch. In fact, I thought about stopping there, but we had a long day as it was."

I was damn glad they hadn't stopped. Especially since I wasn't there. "Wasn't feelin' it tonight." I noticed Darrow was pulling bags out of the back of the SUV and stood to help her. "Let me get those for you."

"Thanks." She looked down at our hands when my finger brushed hers as she handed a couple to me.

"Leave them. I'll bring the rest in," I said when I saw her reach in for more.

"It's okay. I can…"

Her words trailed off when I leveled my gaze on her. It was fairly dark, with just a sliver of the moon illuminating the sky, but I could see her eyes clearly.

"Thank you." She walked to the house, giving me a perfect view of how good her heart-shaped ass looked in her new pair of jeans. Yeah, I was *damn* glad they hadn't stopped at the Long Branch.

I followed her to the back of the house and the bedroom I'd told Z to carry her suitcases to the night before.

"Whose room is this?" she asked when I set her bags on the trunk at the end of the king-size bed.

"Yours now."

"Whose was it before?"

"It was my parents' room."

"Oh."

"It's been a long time since it was, Darrow. Like I said, it's for guests now."

I watched her eyes as they surveyed the space. "I could stay in a smaller one. Wren mentioned that you may have chosen this so I wouldn't be disturbed in the morning, which is actually the last thing I want. I mean, I want to get up when you do and help. I didn't come here on holiday; I hope you know that. I intend to…"

When I rested my hand on her shoulder, she stopped talking and looked up at me. "I'll see you in the morning, Darrow."

I turned and walked out of the room, knowing that if I didn't, I'd do something really stupid, like kiss her. When I walked into the kitchen, Wren was waiting there for me.

"Quint—"

"Save it, Wren."

"You don't know what I was about to say."

"Don't I?" I opened the refrigerator and pulled out a beer. "Want one?"

"Thanks." She took a swig and sat on one of the stools at the kitchen bar. "It's been a long time since I've had a girlfriend. Actually, I can't remember ever having a friend like Darrow."

"She makes you laugh."

Wren smiled. "She does."

"It's nice to hear."

"I'm sorry I haven't been the best company since I came back."

"This is home. You can be any way you want when you're here. Don't feel like talkin' or bein' sociable, you aren't gonna get any grief from me about it."

"I appreciate that, Quint."

"Look, you're my baby sister, and I'd do anything in the world for you, and that includes not making a play for your best friend."

"You want to, though, don't you?"

When Wren smiled, I did too. "Who wouldn't?"

"If you think she's hot, you should see her brother."

I laughed out loud. "I'll take your word for it."

Wren jumped off the stool, walked over, and kissed my cheek. "Good night, Quint."

"'Night, Wren. I'll see you in the morning."

The beautiful woman sleeping in the bedroom on the other side of the wall from mine was responsible for the abrupt yet welcome change in my sister's outlook. No way in hell would I do anything to mess that up. As tempted as I was.

The next morning as I putzed around the kitchen, I found myself hoping that Darrow would come and join me before Wren did, like had happened yesterday. A few minutes later, I was pleasantly surprised when she did.

"Good morning," she said, less sheepishly than the day before.

"Coffee or tea this morning?" I asked.

"I can get it." She reached up to the cupboard from where I'd gotten her one the day before and poured a cup. "You're kidding, right?" she asked, pointing to the bag of grounds sitting near the pot. "Rancher's coffee?"

I smiled. "Yep, strong enough to float a horseshoe."

"What's on the board today?"

"Checking on water. With this heat, we need to make sure the cattle stay hydrated."

"Is that all?"

"It's a big job, but no. We need to do fence checks and look at the health of some of the pastures to see if we need to move the herd."

"What would you like me to do?"

"That's Wren's call."

As soon as I'd said my sister's name, she walked into the kitchen, looking as though she'd been put through the wringer.

"Actually, Quint. I'm not feeling very well. I think it might've been something I ate yesterday. I'm sorry."

"Don't apologize. Go back to bed."

She nodded and shuffled off in the direction from where she came.

"I can just stay here, you know, in case she needs me," said Darrow, not looking me in the eye.

"A minute ago, you were asking what you could do; now you want to hide out in the house?"

Her eyes opened wide, and she shot me a glare. "That isn't what I'm saying. I'm offering so I'm not underfoot. I know I'm not…"

"Not what?" I pressed.

"Never mind."

"Finish your coffee. You'll ride out with me this morning."

"We call this pasture Raptor Ridge," I said when we rode up a crest an hour later.

"Why?"

"Birds of prey."

"I know what raptor means, Quint. What kinds are here?"

"Usually hawks. Every once in a while, we'll see an eagle."

"I've always wanted to see one in the wild."

"You won't this time of year. But you might when the weather turns. Depends on how long you stick around."

"Are you asking?"

I laughed. "Seeing how you just got here two days ago, no, I'm not."

She looked off in the distance at the view from the ridge. "I was telling Wren yesterday that it's really beautiful here."

"I agree. Not everyone thinks so, but I sure do."

I showed her how the grass was getting bare in spots, before leading her over to check the amount of water in the tank.

"We'll move this part of the herd next week and let this pasture revegetate. Probably time to think about separating the first-time calvers and get them ready to put in with the bigger bulls." I waited for her to ask what that meant, but she didn't. I couldn't tell whether it was disinterest, or if she didn't want to appear ignorant. I doubted she knew what I was talking about though.

"When do you start weening the calves?" she asked, surprising me.

"About another two to three weeks."

"And when do they go to market?"

"Depends. Usually end of September or early October."

Darrow nodded.

"You been studying up or something?" I asked, curiosity finally getting the better of me.

"I was out here with Wren for two hours yesterday. What did you think we talked about, the latest Paris fashions?" She smirked and I laughed.

"Quick study."

As she walked over to get back on her horse, her expression grew more serious. "I know you think I'm some silly girl, playing at running away from home, but I'm not, Quint. I don't intend to return to England, and that means I need to figure out how to make my way here in America."

"And you decided cowgirling was your dream job?"

"My real dream job isn't realistic," she mumbled, making me wonder if she was talking more to herself than to me.

"What is it?"

"Not important." She urged her horse away from me even though I hadn't yet told her where we were headed.

"Tell me, Darrow."

"You'll laugh at me," she said over her shoulder.

"Hold up a minute."

She did, and I rode up next to her.

"I won't laugh."

"I want to do what Z does."

I raised a brow, but the last thing I'd do would be to laugh. My sister followed in our father's footsteps to a certain extent, albeit for the United States rather than the UK.

"Why isn't it realistic?"

She sighed. "It just isn't. Can we change the subject please?"

I had no intention of doing so, but I motioned to the west of where we sat on horseback. "We'll head to Schoolhouse next."

She nodded and coaxed Sage from a walk into a trot.

"You might want to follow me," I shouted out to her.

"I was there yesterday. I know my way."

I held Gunsmoke back a minute, marveling at the woman ahead of me. Every hour I spent with her, it seemed, led me to something else I liked about Darrow. She was almost too good to be real.

I continued to hold back, staying close enough that if she started off in the wrong direction, I could shout out and she'd hear me. I didn't need to; she found the pasture completely on her own.

"You have a mighty good memory," I said when we dismounted to check the Schoolhouse water tank.

"I've always had a good sense of direction, I guess."

"Good? You were out here once, and yet you rode straight here."

She shrugged, looking like she was about to say something but changed her mind.

"What?"

She shook her head.

I walked closer to her. "Come on, tell me what you were going to say."

"I had a professor once who told me that while some of my innate abilities were of value, what I lacked in intellectual incisiveness and analytical skills would be my hindrance."

"What does that even mean?"

She laughed. "Precisely."

"Where did you go to school?"

"University? Oxford."

"My mother went to Oxford. It's where she met Z."

"I knew that."

"You remind me of her."

Her mouth dropped open slightly, and her eyebrows went up. "I do?"

"Sure do." I walked over to the tank. The water levels looked good, and so did the grass. This was where we'd move the herd that was now on Raptor Ridge. "There's a line of fence not far from here that we need to check."

She nodded and got back on Sage. We rode for about fifteen minutes, and she didn't say a word.

"You okay?" I asked when we got to the area of the fence that needed to be fixed.

"Yes. Why?"

"You haven't said much since I told you that you remind me of my mother. I hope you know it was a compliment."

Her cheeks blazed a deep red, and she looked away.

"Come on, tell me what you're thinking."

"I'm not thinking anything."

"Liar."

I climbed off Gunsmoke, but she stayed on horseback. I walked over to her and rubbed Sage's muzzle.

"She was smart and beautiful, and she loved to laugh. That's what I remember most about her."

Darrow turned back to look at me; there were tears in her eyes. "Thank you," she whispered.

"What did you think I meant?"

She shook her head.

"If there's any one word that someone might use to describe me, it's stubborn. So if you think I'm going to back off on this, you're wrong."

Her cheeks flamed bright red again. "It wasn't that I thought you meant anything. It's just the nicest thing anyone has ever said to me."

"Then people aren't saying enough nice things to you, and they should."

I studied the horizon where Darrow's gaze rested. More than anything, I wanted to pull her off her horse, take her in my arms, and kiss away her insecurity. I couldn't do that, but even if I could, it was the last thing she needed. How a woman like her could be so insecure baffled me, but the way to shore her up wasn't through romance. I knew that innately. What she needed was someone who saw how capable she was and let her know it. "Let's go." I got back on Gunsmoke and rode toward the ranch house.

6

Darrow

"Where are we going now?" I asked when he rode west.

"I don't know about you, but I'm getting dang hungry. We also need to get you a better pair of gloves and some tools if you're gonna help me fix that fence."

I smiled. "Thank you, Quint."

"You're welcome."

I wondered if he knew why I was thanking him, but it wasn't important. He believed I was there to learn and do, and that's all that mattered.

Wren was still in bed when I checked on her. I came back into the kitchen where Quint had already started cooking.

"She's asleep."

"Probably the best thing for her." He walked over to the refrigerator, opened it, and then closed it again.

"What do you need?"

"We're out of eggs. I thought maybe someone put them in the fridge by mistake, but it doesn't look that way. I'll go out to the coop to get some. Tee-Tee usually does the morning collection, but maybe she needed more down at the bunkhouse."

"I can do it." I waited for him to say something snide, but he didn't.

"Know where the coop is?"

"I don't think it'll be that hard to find. I heard the hens cackling when we rode in."

"Have at it, then."

I stopped on my way out and grabbed my Wellies rather than my work boots.

I closed the door behind me and, with it, let myself smile. I'd proven myself to Quint this morning, at least a little bit. I assumed I had a long way to go, but since today was only my second day to ride out, at least he understood I didn't expect to be waited on.

I made my way over to the coop, pushed the door open, and went in. "Hello, ladies. What have you got for me this morning?" I grabbed one of the wire baskets that sat next to the door and picked up the eggs from nests where no hens were sitting. Then, going one by one, I gently moved each hen sitting on a nest, quietly chattering at them all the while, pulling eggs, and then setting them back down.

"Thank you, ladies," I said, walking back out with over three dozen beautifully colored eggs. I stopped in the mudroom where I saw egg cartons sitting by a utility sink, cleaned each egg, and then put them into the containers. The scent of bacon wafted in my direction, making my stomach growl.

"How'd it go?" Quint asked when I came back in.

I set the cartons on the counter and opened them.

"Wow! Look at all those. Did you clean them?"

I put one hand on my hip. "Of course I cleaned them."

"I know. I was just kidding. Deck came in a little while ago and told me you were singing to the hens. Is that how you got them to give up so many?"

"I wasn't singing to them. I was talking to them. They're a friendly bunch, actually."

Quint laughed, pulled one carton over to the stove, and began cracking them on the griddle. "How do you like them?"

"Any way you fix them. I'm not fussy."

We ate in companionable quiet. I finished before Quint did, so I got up and began cleaning the dishes.

"You don't have to do that," he said, shoveling the last of his breakfast into his mouth.

"I'm happy to. You cooked." Seeing his plate now sat empty, I walked over and picked it up.

"You don't have to come back out with me either if you're not feeling up to it. It's hot as blazes out there, and it's only going to get worse."

"I thought we were going to mend the fence."

"We are. Or I am. I'm just saying I can do it on my own if you've had enough for today."

"I'd rather go back out," I said softly, wondering if maybe I was more of a pest than a helper.

"Better get those dishes done, then." Quint smiled and winked.

We spent all afternoon checking more water tanks and mending more fencing as Quint taught me about the cattle. He also told me when they'd cut their last hay for the season to make sure they were sitting well for the colder winter months when there wouldn't be grass for the herd to feed on.

"That ain't your mama," he said as we watched one calf approach a cow who pushed it away.

"How do they know?" I asked.

"They just do, or in that case, they just don't. Her mama will find her, though."

Within seconds, I saw it happen. "That's amazing."

"I suppose to us, all cows look alike, and to them, all humans do."

"Exactly."

"Should we check on Wren?" I asked a few minutes later.

Quint shook his head. "I sent Tee-Tee a message earlier, and she said she was headed to the house then." He took out his insulated water bottle. "Make sure you stay hydrated."

"You don't have to keep babysitting me. If there are other things you should or want to be doing, I'll understand."

"I don't. To be honest with you, this is a pretty boring time of the year. The heat doesn't help a whole lot. There are afternoons I'd just as soon take a nap than be out here."

"Can you?"

"I suppose, but by the time I got near the barn, I'd probably talk myself out of it. Plus, I'd never hear the end of it from Deck."

I rode just slightly behind him, but far enough away that Sage and Gunsmoke wouldn't get into it. I watched Quint's head survey everything in front of him, and tried to guess what he might be looking for before he turned around to tell me.

"Who do you look like?" I asked at one point, noticing that he didn't favor Z.

"I suppose my mother, or at least I did when I was younger. I got her blonde hair, although as you can see, that's long gone."

"Thank you for today, Quint," I said when we returned to the barn and the horses were cooled down and back in their stalls.

"I enjoyed myself."

"Thanks, but you don't have to lie."

He put his hand on his heart. "Ouch."

I laughed and slugged him like I'd seen Wren do.

"I'd invite you down to the bunkhouse for dinner, but those fellers get pretty wound up at the end of the day."

"It's okay. I can just find something on my own."

"Since Wren is under the weather, why don't we head over to the Branch? They have pretty good food."

"Is that where I'll find out why Deck calls you Fish?"

Quint laughed. "Sure won't."

"You are never going to tell me, are you?"

"We'll see. You might figure it out one day." He looked at his watch. "Meet you back on the porch in thirty?"

"Sounds perfect."

I climbed into the shower and stood under the cool spray. Even though my muscles were stiff, it was too bloody hot to consider warmer water.

When I finished, I stood in front of my wardrobe, trying to decide what to wear. We were just going to get something to eat since Wren didn't feel well. It wasn't a date, and I didn't want him to think I thought it was.

My first choice was a loose-fitting sundress, but I decided that was far too date-y. It was too hot to wear trousers—or jeans—and the shorts I had seemed a little too sexy.

"Bugger it," I said, pulling out one of the dresses.

7

Quint

Since I was ten minutes ahead of schedule, I grabbed a beer before heading out to the porch. I hadn't rushed. In fact, if I were going to the Branch with Deck, I would've been ready ten minutes earlier still.

I'd peeked in on Wren, who said she was feeling better, but added that the idea of food would make her turn green again.

I took a long swig, hoping that Deck wouldn't show himself tonight, at least while Darrow and I were there eating.

Hearing footsteps, I turned around when she came out the door, and almost dropped my beer.

Her hair was loose and hung in soft curls down her back. She had on a little yellow dress that rested mid-thigh, and her long legs were tucked into a pair of shorty cowgirl boots embroidered with flowers. If I didn't know better, I would've guessed she was straight outta Texas.

At first, I'd pulled out a plain t-shirt to wear, but now was glad that I'd changed my mind and wore a short-sleeved, pearl-snap Rockmount shirt instead.

"Ready?" she asked, taking the bottle from my hand and pulling her own swig.

When she handed it back, I finished what was left of it, set it on the table, and led her over to my truck.

"You look mighty pretty tonight, Darrow," I said as she climbed up on the running board. I couldn't help but breathe in her scent, which seemed completely natural. No perfume needed with this woman.

She smiled and tucked her dress under her bottom, all ladylike, before she sat on the seat. "You look mighty handsome yourself, Quint."

Instead of walking around the front of my truck, I went around the back, giving myself time to roll my shoulders. This woman hadn't been in Texas three days, and here we were, going out to dinner alone, her in a dress, me in a pearl-snap. If that wasn't date attire, I didn't know what was. On top of that, I'd told her she looked pretty, and she reciprocated. That, ladies and gentlemen, was called flirting, and I wasn't supposed to be doing it.

Before I got into the truck, I gave myself a pep talk, determined to rein way in.

Of course that resolve went all to hell as soon as she looked over at me and smiled.

I pulled up in front of the hundred-year-old saloon and put the truck in park. There were plenty of open spaces, but three or four hours from now, the place would be packed. Most of the cowboys were away at ranch rodeos on the weekend this time of year, which meant Thursday night would be the Long Branch's busiest.

I walked around and opened Darrow's door, holding out my hand to help her down.

"Thank you," she murmured and then put her hand on her stomach. "Oh my God, what is that?"

"What do you mean?" Shit, was she getting sick like Wren was?

"That smell. It's heavenly."

I had to admit, there was little that smelled better than a big ol' steak on a fired-up grill after being out on the ranch all day long. "If I had to guess, I'd say it was a T-bone."

"That's what I'm having."

I wouldn't spoil her fun by telling her that the steak was bigger than she was.

We got a table across from the bar, and I sat where I could keep watch on every cowboy that walked in and eyed her up. If one craned their neck a little too long, I'd shoot a glare their way, and if one dared approach the table, I'd send a death ray in their direction.

The Branch wasn't the kind of place that had menus. If you didn't know what they offered, you probably didn't belong in these parts.

I saw the bartender, a man I'd known almost all my life, sauntering over to take our order.

"You still want that T-bone?" I asked.

"Um, sure."

"Beer okay?"

"Perfect."

"Mind if I just order for the both of us?"

"Have at it, cowboy."

Goddamn, did she have to keep smiling at me that way? And that accent, *shit,* it made me want to carry her back out to my truck and go find some quiet country road where I could kiss the daylights out of her.

"Hey, Bobby. We're ready to order."

Bobby raised a brow.

"Two T-bones, medium rare, loaded bakers, and two long necks."

"You got it. Anything else, Mr. Alexander?"

I shook my head and laughed. "That'll do it, Mr. MacIver."

"I take it you know him," said Darrow when Bobby left the table, chuckling.

"Since we were kids."

"Cheers," she said when Bobby came back with the two bottles of beer. "I like this place. Thanks for bringing me here."

I looked around the bar with its wood plank flooring covered in sawdust and the barstools with red leather seats that were so old the stuffing had come out through the cracks. "You sure about that?"

"What? That I like it? I don't. I love it."

"Lookin' pretty old and tired to me."

"You Yanks. Calling a place old that's been around, what? A hundred years?"

I nodded.

"The pub closest to the abbey, that my mates and I frequent, has been around since the 1200s."

"You're kidding."

"I'm not."

"I'd like to see that place."

"Seeing as I don't plan to return to England, I guess you'll have to get someone else to be your tour guide."

I leaned forward when she rested against the tall back of the booth. "Why aren't you going back?"

"It's a long story."

I motioned to Bobby, who nodded. "Bring us a bucket."

Darrow's eyebrow raised, and I knew damn well she wanted to ask, but I also knew damn well she wouldn't. A minute later, Bobby dropped a bucket on our table, with ten more long necks set in ice.

"We got all night and plenty of beer. Let's hear it."

"Only if you tell me why Deck calls you Fish."

I sat back. "I promise, when the time is right, you'll know. But trust that if I tell you, it won't be nearly as good as you seeing for yourself."

That intrigued her, I could tell. Those sweet dimpled cheeks of hers were flaming bright red.

"My story pales in comparison, then, I'm afraid."

I looked into her eyes, knowing I was way beyond simple flirting. I wanted to know everything about this woman. Why she didn't want to go back to England, why she thought her dream job was unrealistic, and most especially, how she'd look with that long dark hair spread out on my lily-white sheets while I spent hours getting acquainted with her naked body. "Tell me anyway," I said in my most cowboy-like voice.

"I promise you it isn't that interesting."

"Tell me and I'll be the judge."

"You see, the reason is that when I'm in England, I'm not very interesting."

"I don't believe that nonsense for a minute."

"It's true. I'm the daughter of the fourteenth Duke of Bedfordshire and sister of the fifteenth, who was also a high-ranking MI6 agent. That same brother is married to a woman who was a former Russian assassin. They met when she was hired to kill him. Now they're married and have two children."

She looked up at me after playing with the label on her beer bottle the entire time she spoke.

"Go on."

"Isn't that enough?"

I took a long drink, set my empty bottle on the table, and folded my hands.

"Okay, but you'll soon be falling asleep."

I didn't say a word, nor did my expression change.

"As it turns out, my father had an affair with one of the scullery maids before he married my mother, which culminated in the birth of a son. In exchange for a lofty position with MI6, my mother—you caught that part, right? My mother arranged for Sir Ranald Caird, her beau at the time, to marry the pregnant maid so she, my mother, could one day be Duchess of Bedfordshire. After my father's death, two things happened. The child that Sir Caird raised with the former maid went positively mad and tried to kill both of my brothers, and well, blow up the entirety of the abbey. Oh, and the Russian assassin along with my nephew—a baby at the time—and myself, were used as bait to lure my brothers into his trap."

I raised a brow.

"See?"

"What's the rest of the story?"

"Well, then, my other brother, Sutton, fell in love with your sister. I'm not sure what happened there, because neither of them will speak of it, but whatever the story is, I'm sure it's interesting."

"Why are you here, Darrow?"

"Because when I'm there, I get lost."

"What does that mean?"

"Conversations take place around me as if I'm too thick to understand what everyone else is talking about." She sighed and blinked away the tears in her eyes. "I'm feeling sorry for myself now," she whispered.

"No, you're not. You're telling me why you left."

"The final straw was when my boyfriend, who also works for MI5—oh, wait, did I tell you that Sutton is now the interim chief of MI6?"

I shook my head. "Tell me about the boyfriend."

"He's known me my whole bloody life." She looked away, and as much as I wanted her to look at me when she told me the thing that was hardest for her, I gave her the space to do it her way.

"I told him. Hypothetically, of course."

"That you wanted to work for MI6?"

She nodded, but still didn't look at me. "Not me, per se."

I wasn't sure what that meant, but it didn't matter. "How did he react?"

"As though it was the most ridiculous thing he'd ever heard."

I reached across the table and took her hand.

"I'm a decoration," she said, a tear rolling down her cheek. "My job is to look pretty, be prepared to speak when spoken to, on any number of subjects, even though whomever I'm conversing with doesn't bother to even listen to my response."

"You and the boyfriend…what happened?"

"I told him to sod off, but it wasn't just that he didn't take me seriously about MI6. In fact, I don't think he was even listening to me. But there was more. He turned into someone who treated me the same way everyone else did. Like I didn't have a brain in my head." She turned her head and looked at me. "I went to bloody Oxford. They don't just let anyone in, you know."

"I do know. So why here?"

"Your sister. She was the first person who talked to me, confided in me, included me, when no one else did. She never assumed I was thick as a plank."

"Because you're not. You're one of the brightest, most interesting people I've ever met."

"Give it time. You'll see. As soon as the pale is off the rose, you'll find me as boring as everyone else does."

"That would never happen."

"As they say, never say never."

Bobby approached the table, carrying two enormous platters of food. When he set one in front of Darrow, she looked at me, her eyes as big as saucers, and burst out laughing.

"Why didn't you tell me I was ordering an entire cow?"

I laughed too. "It's what you wanted. You should always get what you want, Darrow. You deserve it."

The smile left her face, and she lowered her gaze. "You're being nice, and I appreciate it—"

I reached over and put my fingers on her chin. "Look at me." I waited until she did. "In the short time I've had the pleasure to know you, you've impressed me at every turn. You're aware of every single thing happening around you. Things it took me years to learn, you pick up in an afternoon. You probably understand more about ranching than I do because you're that smart."

"Quint, you don't have to do this."

"I'm not doing anything except stating the truth. Whoever can't see it the way I do, doesn't deserve you in their life."

My voice was tinged with anger because I was. Darrow Whittaker was everything I could ever imagine wanting a woman to be, and yet whoever this asshole was that called himself her boyfriend, made her doubt herself so much that she'd left home to create a different life.

"Should we invite the rest of the bar over to join us? We have enough food to feed them all."

"You may want to share yours, but there's no way they're getting any of mine."

"You can't eat all of that."

"You don't think so? Watch me."

8

Darrow

I couldn't believe it, but Quint was true to his word. He not only ate all of this steak, but finished the potato too. I'd quit eating at least ten minutes ago, my stomach full, and yet it didn't look as though I'd eaten ten percent of my meal.

"It's a terrible waste," I said.

"Don't worry, it'll get eaten."

My eyes opened wide. "You're joking."

Quint laughed out loud. "Not by me. At least not this time."

"Thank you, Quint. I really enjoyed myself tonight. And today."

"It isn't over yet."

"No?"

"Ever line-danced?"

"Can't say as I have."

"Then, you will tonight."

"I'm not a good dancer."

"Right. And you're not very interesting either."

I laughed. "I'm serious. I'll step on your feet."

"Not when we line-dance, darlin'."

I was so tired I almost fell asleep on the ride home, but it had been a wonderful day. I'd enjoyed the time I spent riding the ranch, and then our time at dinner even more. I'd been the one insisting we stay and dance longer once I got the hang of it. I'd felt like Cinderella, knowing that soon the clock would strike midnight and we'd have to leave, but I wanted to squeeze out every bit of fun I could before that happened. My face even hurt from smiling as much as I had.

Quint made me feel so special, and for that, I couldn't thank him enough.

He pulled up in front of the ranch house, turned the ignition off, and came around to open my door. He held out his hand to help me out, but something felt different about him. He was no longer smiling, and even though his hand touched mine, he felt a million miles away.

"Is everything okay?"

"Yep. It's all good. Let's get you inside, and then I have some things to check on in the barn."

"I can help—"

"Not tonight, Darrow."

"Right. Of course. Well, thank you for dinner. I had a lovely time. Good night." I stalked away from him, hoping he wouldn't follow, and he didn't.

Once inside, I went straight to the bedroom and closed the door behind me before my tears began to fall. Had it all been some kind of act to make me feel good? If so, he couldn't have just continued it until I was safely inside?

God, I felt like such an idiot. There I was, floating on air the whole way home, only to have my bubble burst the minute he turned off the engine of his truck.

I took a shower, crawled into bed, and was about to set the alarm on my phone, but stopped myself. There was no way I could face Quint in the morning, especially if Wren was still under the weather.

He spent enough time trying to convince me that my help wasn't necessary, I might as well listen and sleep in tomorrow.

Even though I woke at dawn the next morning, I didn't get out of bed. I rolled over and tried to go back to sleep, but after tossing about for over a half hour, I got up. Quint would be on his way to the barn by now anyway.

I went into the kitchen, determined to have a cup of tea since there'd be no one there judging me for it.

"Good morning," said Wren when she walked in.

"Hi. How are you feeling?"

"Much, much better. Thanks. I think the salad I ordered at lunch the other day was bad. You were smart to have the soup."

I looked over at the empty coffee pot. Quint hadn't left me any? I hadn't planned to drink it, but still.

"I was thinking we could go into San Antonio today, maybe do some shopping, play tourists, and even stay for dinner. If we don't feel like driving back, there's a wonderful little inn right on the river. We could just stay over."

"Oh. Isn't there work to be done today?" Or was it just that Quint didn't want me underfoot and told his sister to get me out of there? I turned my back to Wren, afraid I was about to cry.

"Quint, Decker, and some of the other hands left for Big Bend, so no. We have the day off. The whole week-end, actually."

"Big Bend?"

"The ranch rodeo. King-Alexander has a team that competes almost every weekend. Quint and Deck compete in team roping plus some other events. Team roping is their best, though."

We spent hours and hours talking yesterday and last night, and he hadn't once mentioned he'd be gone the entire weekend. Hadn't even thought to, the previous night when he couldn't get away from me fast enough.

"San Antonio sounds lovely. Would we have to come back tomorrow or could we stay longer?"

"We can stay as long as you'd like. Quint humors me by letting me help out, but he doesn't really need me. Half the time, I'm sure Deck is annoyed as hell that I'm around."

I nodded. I understood completely. Only it wasn't just Deck who was annoyed by me; Quint was too.

9

Quint

"What the hell is your problem?" Deck shouted at me.

"Nothing."

"Bullshit. You've never broken a barrier in your life."

"Big fuckin' deal, Deck. So I did now. *Jesus,* it happens all the time."

"You've been a dick all day long. What the hell happened last night?"

"Leave it alone, Decker."

The man giving me a ton of shit at the moment and I had been best friends since we were kids. Along with managing the ranching part of the operation, Decker was the head of security for King-Alexander. He had as much training in intelligence as Z and Wren did, although in this case, it wouldn't take a spy to figure out what my problem was.

"Fine. The guys and I are goin' to the saloon. You comin' along, or are you gonna stay here and sulk?"

"Go on ahead and I'll catch up."

Decker shook his head and walked away, and I was glad for it. I didn't need anyone else telling me I was off my game. Breaking the barrier wasn't really that big of a deal. As a roping team, we were penalized ten seconds because I went through the rope stretched across the box before the steer. Rules were it was supposed to break the barrier first in order to give it a ten-second head start.

It hadn't really mattered in the end, because I hadn't roped the steer anyway.

Was it the only time we were eliminated in the first round? Hell, no. Was it the first time we were eliminated because I shouldn't have been competing anyway? Yep.

Last night had been one of the best of my life. Some might think I was overstating it if I were to say it out loud, which I never would. But it had been. Darrow was everything I told her she was and more.

She was damn smart, had a quick wit, and a smile that lit up everything around her. Sure, she was beautiful, but she was so much more than that.

It was the drive home from the Branch that had sobered me up, not from the booze, but from the headiness of spending an entire day and evening with her.

Under any other circumstance, I would have invited her into my bed. There was no doubt in my mind that having her naked body next to mine, burying myself in her warmth, kissing her like I'd longed to do every minute I was with her, would have been spectacular. Mind-blowingly so.

I could only imagine the conversation Darrow had with Wren this morning. I cringed thinking about the earful my sister would give me when I got home on Sunday. I'd say it was none of her damn business, but she'd warned me to leave Darrow alone, and while I hadn't made a move on her, I'd all but done so.

We were halfway home last night when I thought about telling Darrow I was leaving in the morning, but then wondered why I would. She wasn't there to spend time with me; she was there to see Wren and to "start a new life." I wasn't going to be a part of that life, so why insinuate myself now?

"Hey, Quint," I heard a quiet voice say. I looked up at the cute barrel racer I'd hooked up with from time to time.

"Hey, Kayleigh."

"You goin' over to the saloon?"

"Not tonight, darlin'."

"You want some company?"

I didn't. The only company I wanted was back at my ranch, and even if I was there with her right now, I had no business keeping it.

"Sorry, sweetheart. I won't be good company for anyone tonight."

"Everyone breaks barriers, Quint."

I nodded.

"Okay, then. Maybe I'll see you tomorrow."

I tipped my hat. I hadn't even bothered to stand when the woman approached. My mama would be ashamed of me for that.

Instead of popping open another beer, I went into the trailer and poured myself a glass of whiskey. I threw some ice in it, not because I liked it that way, but maybe it would slow me down a bit. I wouldn't be driving anywhere tonight, but if I got drunk, Lord knew what kind of other mistakes I might make.

By the time we left Big Bend on Sunday, everyone on our team was in a foul mood, and it all stemmed from me. I'd been surly and, quite frankly, an asshole. We didn't place in a single event, and after my disastrous out on Friday night, I didn't even bother entering any.

I hoped Decker would ride home in one of the other trucks, but right before we pulled out, he got in with me.

"Never known you to just give up," he said when we were an hour into our drive.

"Leave me alone, Deck. Everyone deserves to have a bad go without getting constant shit for it."

"And if that's all it was, you wouldn't be hearin' a word about it. This is different. You aren't yourself. One day, who cares. Three days? Somethin's wrong."

I looked off at the horizon that stretched ahead of us. Once we pulled through the ranch gates, I intended to continue to make myself scarce. Better to tell Deck that now than to have him question me in front of potential witnesses.

"Darrow is here mainly because of a bad breakup, and while I normally wouldn't pay any attention to shit like that, I think she's lookin' to rebound with me, and that can't happen. God knows how long she'll be at the ranch, and when things go south, which we both know they will, what the hell do I do then? Not to mention, Wren would put my balls in a vise."

"I could take her off your hands if it will help."

"You lay one fucking hand—" I stopped short when I saw the look on Deck's face.

"That's what I thought," he said.

"You're an asshole."

"Pretty sure you got me beat there."

We were almost home before I spoke again. "I'm gonna be takin' a few days off."

"Where you headed?"

"Don't know yet."

Deck nodded. "Let me know if there's anything I can do besides run the whole damn operation while you go off and hide like a scared bunny rabbit."

I didn't respond. There was no point in getting mad; that's what Deck was after.

"What do I say when Wren asks where you went off to?"

"Tell her I went to see a man about a horse."

10

Darrow

When Quint came home a week later, it was as though our night at the Long Branch had never happened. In fact, it was as if he hadn't spent any time with me at all. He was polite, but that was the extent of it.

The first couple of days, I came out of my room when I heard him in the kitchen, hoping we could at least have a conversation. Both days he'd finished his coffee, told me to have a good day, and walked out.

The third day, I waited until I was sure he was already gone before going out and making myself a cup of tea, like I had every day that he was gone.

Wren and I had gotten accustomed to checking with Decker about what needed to be done each morning. He never went easy on us. Often, my hands were blistered by the end of the day, but I wouldn't tell Wren that let alone Quint. Not that he paid any attention to me.

At first, he ate dinner with the guys at the bunk-house, but after Wren mentioned it, he and sometimes Decker started joining us. He rarely spoke unless asked a direct question, and even then he kept his responses to as few words as possible.

By the next week, when Quint came home from yet another weekend rodeo and his behavior was no different than when he left, I was fed up. Instead of spending each day feeling unwelcome, I decided to visit friends who were in the Washington, DC, area. The situation wasn't such that I could stay for more than a day or two. I'd decide between now and then whether I'd go back to England from there.

That night at dinner, I decided to broach the subject since Deck hadn't joined us. "I want to thank you for your generosity and hospitality." Both Wren and Quint stopped eating and looked at me. "I've decided it's time for me to move on, but I can't tell you how much I've enjoyed my time here."

"What do you mean?" Wren asked at the same time Quint said, "Where are you going?"

I looked between them. "I have friends on the East Coast who have invited me to visit. From there, I'm not certain what I'll do, but whatever it is, will be a grand adventure." I'd plastered a fake smile on my face so often in the last three weeks, it almost felt normal. As long as I didn't have to say anything more, I might be able to keep up my ruse.

Quint got up from the table and took his dishes to the kitchen even though it was obvious he wasn't finished eating. Moments later, I heard the back door close.

"I don't understand," said Wren.

I squared my shoulders. All I had to do was convince Wren that I wasn't cut out for a life I'd grown to love more each day.

"I have to admit this is much more difficult work than I ever dreamed," I began.

Wren threw her napkin on her unfinished meal. "Stiff upper lip and all that, right?"

She'd hit the nail on the head. "I don't know what you mean," I lied.

"What's really going on? I won't relent until you tell me the truth."

Wren's statement reminded me of the day with Quint when he told me that he was stubborn enough not to give up until I told him why I'd left England.

"It's Quint, isn't it?"

"No—"

Wren stood up and put her hands on her hips. "What happened between the two of you?"

"I don't know what you mean," I repeated. How many times could I use that line?

"First, he disappears for a week without any explanation. Now, you're leaving. I was sick for one damn day. *What happened*?"

God, what was I doing? The woman had been nothing but nice to me, even letting me stay on for a month after I'd shown up unannounced. "I'm sorry," I began, putting my hand on Wren's wrist. "If you'll sit back down, I'll tell you."

I told her about our day and how we'd gone to dinner that night. "We talked for hours and danced, and had what I thought was a wonderful evening, but on the way back to the ranch, it was as though a switch flipped. Quint went from magnanimous to withdrawn. The next morning, he was gone, and well, you know what's happened from there."

"I see. So why are you leaving?"

"Isn't it obvious? I've made the poor man uncomfortable in his own home, for God's sake."

"I'll talk to him."

"Please don't. I've honestly had enough humiliation for one year. Let me leave with my head held high, I beg of you."

"But I'm going to miss you so much."

"I'll miss you too." When I saw a tear run down Wren's cheek, I couldn't hold mine back any longer. "Maybe you could come to DC?"

Wren shook her head. "I can't."

I almost asked why not, but thought better of it. If the woman said she couldn't, there must be a good reason for it.

11

Quint

I stood just inside the back door, eavesdropping on every word Darrow said to my sister. I could tell by her voice at the last bit that she was crying.

When Darrow arrived, it was like a light went back on inside of Wren, and now, because of me, it would go out again. I couldn't let that happen. I had to figure out a way to get Darrow to stay without letting on that I'd heard their conversation while at the same time not leading her on like I had the night we went to the Branch.

The hardest part, and the reason I avoided talking to Darrow as much as I did, was I feared if I had even a simple conversation with her, I'd let on how I really felt.

It wasn't just for Wren's sake that I wanted Darrow to stay. I lived for every time I caught a glimpse of her smile. She didn't know it, but several times a day, I'd go and check on them, always staying far enough away that neither Darrow nor Wren would spot me.

I'd berated Decker for working her too hard, especially when I saw her standing at the sink in the barn, running her blistered hands under cold water to ease the pain.

I'd believed that by keeping my distance, she'd forget about me. Like Wren said, it was one damn day. It didn't matter that it was a day I would never forget.

I eased the door open and went out to the porch as quietly as I could and sat in the darkness. I saw Decker inside the brightly lit barn, but I needed time to think on my own, so I stayed where I was, wishing that I'd grabbed a beer.

A few minutes later, Wren came out and joined me. "I thought you might like one of these." She handed me a bottle.

"You read my mind."

"Quint, I want to talk to you about Darrow."

"She asked you not to."

Wren paused but then smiled. "You heard us."

"Chickenshit move, but yeah, I only pretended to leave."

"I was wrong to interfere. I know you're a good man, Quint."

I looked up at my sister. "I'm not, Wren. Not when it comes to Darrow. You were right to warn me away."

"Why are you saying that? What would you—"

"I'd want everything from her. Everything. I would take her and possess her and never want to let her go. I bet I could talk her into staying here, and that would be the absolute worst thing that could happen. She wants more out of life than what I could offer. A lot more, in fact."

"You're being awfully melodramatic."

"Am I?" I took a long swig of my beer and then stood. "Mark my words, Wren."

Three days later, I was sitting at the dinner table, thinking about everything I still had to do that night in order to leave for the first of the team roping qualifiers for the World Championships in November.

So far I'd heard no further mention of Darrow's departure, but what in the hell would I do if I left tomorrow and she was gone when I got back on Sunday?

When we finished eating, Wren stood to clear the dishes. When Darrow got up to help, my sister playfully pushed her back into her chair. "I'll get it. You can relax tonight."

"There's a team roping qualifier this weekend you might be interested in seein'," I said to Darrow before I talked myself out of it.

She immediately looked over at Wren. "That sounds like fun. Wren, do you want to go?"

If there was ever a single time in my life I wanted my sister to play along with me, this was it.

I breathed a silent sigh of relief when I heard Wren say, "I'd love to, sweetie, but I have that report I have to finish up."

"Report?" I mouthed, making sure Darrow didn't turn around and catch me.

"Oh, well…"

"You should go," pushed Wren. "It's a lot of fun, and Quint and his partner are ranked pretty high this year."

"If you're sure."

"Positive," said Wren, winking at me behind Darrow's back.

"Thanks," I mouthed to Wren and then turned to Darrow. "We'll leave tomorrow right after morning chores. Be ready to go by eight or so."

She nodded. "What should I bring?"

I leaned forward. "I wouldn't mind any if you brought that pretty yellow dress and those sweet shorty boots along."

"Also bring jeans and work boots," Wren added. "Quint, you'll want her to see everything that goes on behind the scenes too. That's more than half the fun."

I excused myself from the table and went out to the barn. As I'd expected, Decker was already loading our gear.

"There's been a development."

"Oh, yeah? What's that?" Deck asked without looking up.

"Darrow is coming along."

"Guess I'll be sleepin' with the horses." Deck growled, but I caught a glimpse of his smile.

"You can sleep where you always do. Darrow won't be sleeping in the trailer."

Decker laughed. "Right."

12

Darrow

When the sun rose the next morning, I was still wide awake. I'd been stunned last night when Quint invited me to go to the rodeo and even more so when Wren made up an excuse as to why she couldn't go along. I couldn't believe they thought I didn't see the unspoken messages going back and forth between brother and sister.

Once in bed, I started overthinking everything from the abruptness of the invitation to the weirdness of Wren's response. What kept me awake all night, though, was my worry that what had happened between Quint and me the last time would happen again. If it did, I'd be on a plane back to England the day after we got home from the rodeo.

There was no way I could go through that uncertainty again. He'd hurt me, and the minute I'd gotten used to the ways things would be from then on, Quint invited me to spend the weekend with him.

That was what he was doing, wasn't it? Or was he just inviting me to go along to help? I knew there was another woman who was part of the team. When Wren had told me that a few days ago, I immediately assumed that had been the reason for Quint's sudden personality change the night he and I had gone out. It all made sense until Wren added that she was the fiancée of one of the other team members.

If he had invited me along only to work, wouldn't he have said so? Wouldn't either he or Deck tell me what they expected of me?

On the other hand, why would Quint tell me to bring "that pretty yellow dress" if it wasn't something more.

"Argh," I growled, looking up at the ceiling. These thoughts rolled around in my head all night long, and I still wasn't any closer to figuring out what Quint's motive was.

"Knock, knock," I heard Wren's voice at my door.

"Come in." I sat up in bed.

"I brought you some tea." Wren walked over and handed me the cup.

"Thank you." I wished she had brought me coffee instead. After the first few times I'd had what Quint brewed in the morning, I got used to it. The only reason I went back to drinking tea was because I was mad at him.

"Are you all set?"

"I don't know." I got out of bed and walked over to the clothes I'd laid out. "What do you think?"

Wren looked at the mess on the trunk. "Take this, but not this," she said, separating everything from one pile into two. "I'll be right back," she said after more than half of my clothes were moved to the "don't take" side.

She came back with an armful of garments that were far dressier than what I'd picked out.

"Half the fun of going is at the parties every night. You'll want to dress up a little for those."

"I have this one," I said, holding up the yellow dress.

Wren took it and held it up to me. "I like that one a lot." She moved it back over to the "take pile" and held up a dress of hers that was pink. "What do you think of this one?"

"I love it, but you haven't even worn it yet." I pointed to the price tag that still hung from the sleeve.

"All the better. Quint hasn't seen it before."

Wren had also brought two more pairs of jeans and two more shirts.

"We're only going to be gone two days."

"There are morning events, afternoon events, and then the other stuff at night. You'll want to change for each one. In between, you may be in the barns, which you'll also change for."

"You've got to be kidding."

Wren put one hand on her hip. "Listen, Quint is my brother, and I've been to plenty of these ranch rodeos. There are more women at these things who are trying to catch his eye than I can count. Who knows, maybe you're not out to impress him. If that's the case, take what you picked out before. If, on the other hand, you want to show these women up, take what I'm giving you."

I snapped Wren's clothes out of her hands and began rolling them to put in my trunk.

"That's what I thought." She winked. "Here," she said, handing me one of the pair of jeans she'd brought in. "Wear these so you can help unload."

I put my hand on Wren's. "Thank you for doing this. I know you don't really have a report to work on."

"You picked up on that, huh?"

I nodded and smiled.

"My brother is a good man. He may try to say otherwise, but he is. I want you to have a good time this weekend, Darrow."

I wanted that too. I only prayed that when it was all over, Quint didn't disappear again.

I checked my watch for the fourth time in as many minutes. It was a little after seven. Quint had said we'd leave at eight. Maybe I should wheel my trunk out to the porch and wait there. Or would that make me look too anxious? Thank God Wren had suggested I wear jeans. I probably wouldn't have, and what message might that have sent?

"Argh," I growled again. Why was I doing this to myself? If only I hadn't had dinner with Quint that night, I wouldn't be so nervous now.

"Everything okay in here?"

I sprung off the bed when Quint stepped into the room. "Fine. Everything is fine. Are we ready to go? Sorry, I should've wheeled my trunk out. I don't know what I was thinking. You know, maybe I should—"

Quint walked over and put a finger on my lips. "I will take care of your, uh…trunk. No, you shouldn't have wheeled it out. We aren't leaving for another half hour, and breakfast is ready and waiting in the kitchen. Before you say anything on that subject, I want you to know that Tee-Tee brought over some of her breakfast burritos earlier, and they're being kept warm in the oven. Okay?"

His finger was still on my lips, so I nodded.

"Finally, I want you to know how glad I am that you're going along this weekend. The other thing I want you to know is that I'm sorry the stupid way I acted has resulted in you being so nervous around me."

"I've always been nervous around you," I whispered when he moved his fingers away.

"I'm even sorrier for that."

"Quint? What happened that night?"

For a minute, I thought he was leaving when he walked over to the bedroom door. Instead, he closed it and returned to where I stood.

"I had an amazing time with you that night. Better than any other night I can remember. You yourself told me that you were here in part because your previous relationship ended. If I hadn't backed off, I might've done something neither of us was ready for."

"I wanted you to."

He cupped my cheek. "I know you did, and while I didn't handle it right, we're both better off now because nothing happened between us then."

I took a step back. "I'm worried it's going to happen again."

He took my hand in his. "I promise it won't."

"What is this, exactly? Am I going to the rodeo to help with the team? Or am I going with you?"

Instead of answering, Quint brought his other hand to my cheek and looked into my eyes before leaning in to kiss me. What started off as a soft, sweet kiss, quickly became harder, more heated when I put my arms around his neck and kissed him back.

He didn't pull away until we both heard Wren's footsteps in the hallway.

"Does that answer your question?" he asked, resting his forehead against mine.

"Pretty much."

When he took a step back, I was afraid I would crumble into a heap on the floor. In the history of kisses

I'd experienced in my lifetime, that was by far the hottest. I hoped Quint didn't ask me more questions, because I wasn't sure I could speak let alone think. What had he said? Something about breakfast?

"Darrow, are you okay?"

"Um, yeah. Can we go eat now?"

13

Quint

God, this woman made me smile. I motioned for her to go ahead in part so I could watch her sweet bottom sashay in her tight jeans.

And that kiss? Lord Almighty. It was enough to make me keep the bedroom door locked and back her up against the bed. If Deck and the rest of the crew wouldn't be waiting on us to leave in less than an hour, I might've been more tempted, but I didn't want the first time she and I were together to be rushed. And I sure as hell planned to be with the gorgeous Miss Whittaker. It might not be tonight, or even this weekend, but I knew it would be soon. I wouldn't be able to keep my hands off her much longer. When she said she'd wanted me to "do something neither of us was ready for," I knew she was feeling the same way I was. The kiss only drove that point home further.

When we walked into the kitchen, Wren was waiting with her back up against the counter. I could guess by the look on her face that she knew what had just happened back in the bedroom. Thank God she was smiling.

I opened the oven, pulled out three of Tee-Tee's breakfast burritos, and put each one on a plate. "Have a seat," I said to both of them.

"You are going to love these," Wren said to Darrow. "They're almost as good as her margaritas."

I wasn't positive, but I thought I saw her flinch at the mention of another night I'd behaved badly. Later, when we were alone, I'd remind myself to apologize for that too.

"There are more if you'd like another," I said, noticing Darrow had already finished eating what was on her plate.

"Are you sure?"

I smiled and stood.

"I can get it."

"Let me," I said, noticing the smirk that still sat on my sister's face.

After we finished eating, Wren offered to clean up what little mess we'd made so Darrow and I could get on the road.

"Have fun," Wren said, winking at both of us, which of course caused Darrow's cheeks to flame the adorable way they did when she was embarrassed.

I led her over to the truck that sat waiting with the trailer already hitched and loaded. I opened the passenger door and held out my hand to help her in. As I breathed in her scent, I longed to lean forward and taste her lips one more time before I got behind the wheel. The drive would take us a good solid three hours, and I'd hunger for her the whole way.

Instead of getting all the way in and sitting down, Darrow stopped, put her arms around my neck, and kissed me the same way I'd just been thinking of doing to her.

I put my hand on the back of her neck, holding her tight so she couldn't back away before I was ready. The kiss went on and on, until I heard the rest of my team whistling and catcalling.

Darrow backed away when I released her neck, and took a seat in the truck. I leaned forward and kissed her bright-red cheek. "I love how your skin flames when you're embarrassed."

The way she smiled and dropped her gaze made me want to take her right there in the driveway. This was going to be a damn long drive.

We had the radios on between trucks, and since no one in the caravan said they needed to stop along the way, we drove straight through to Bluebell Creek, where the rodeo would start later that day.

Everyone pitched in to get unloaded, including Darrow, and when we were finished, we had a couple of hours to kill before we had to get ready for that night's events.

"I'm going to get Darrow settled in over at the cabin," I told Deck.

"That's right. I forgot all about that place. Guess that's why I get the rig all to myself tonight."

"Don't get any ideas. I'll be here with you," I said when I made sure Darrow was out of earshot.

"I'd lay heavy odds you won't be."

"Quit, Deck," I growled when I saw Darrow approaching.

"What do we do now?" she asked in that sexy voice that stirred me up.

I glared at Decker, who smirked and walked away. "The King family has a cabin here on Bluebell Creek. That's where you'll be staying tonight."

"Oh," she murmured, those sweet cheeks flaming bright.

"We'll talk about it on the way." I helped her into the truck, but because she hadn't hesitated to kiss me earlier, I pulled her off the seat. "I kind of liked the way you thanked me last time," I said before covering her mouth with mine.

I kissed her more deeply than before and cupped her bottom, giving it a squeeze before I let her go.

"You can't really expect me to sleep alone after that," she said, climbing back into the truck and pushing me away so she could close the door.

I laughed and walked around the front of the truck, my eyes on her the whole way. When I got in and saw she'd slid to the center of the bench seat, I remembered why I'd special ordered it that way instead of with the standard bucket seats. After I put the vehicle in gear and steered us out of the crowded field where the other competitors were still busy setting up, I rested my hand on Darrow's thigh.

"I sure am glad you agreed to come along this weekend."

"Not half as glad as I am, cowboy," she answered, turning toward me and reaching up to plant a kiss on my neck.

I tightened my grip on her thigh and slid my hand farther up, closer to the heat I felt emanating from between her legs. "If it weren't a qualifying event," I groaned, "I sure as hell wouldn't be competing tonight."

She grinned. "Why ever not?"

"Because once we get to the cabin later tonight, I'm not going to want to leave it again until I've learned every inch of your sweet body."

"Mmm," she moaned. "I guess you didn't bring me along just to help."

I stopped the truck, took it out of gear, and released my seat belt. I turned toward Darrow and put my hand on the back of her neck. "I need more," I murmured before kissing her one more time.

I let her go and started the truck up again. The sooner I got her to the cabin, the quicker I could kiss her without an audience.

"This is so beautiful," she said when I pulled up next to the building that was used more for fishing and hunting than romance. I should've thought to ask one of my cousins to come and clean it up when I called to see if I could use it this weekend.

"I have to warn you before we go inside, the cabin is mostly used by a bunch of old guys. It might need to be cleaned up a little."

"Then, that's what we'll do," she said, smiling.

"You're always so agreeable."

"No. I'm not, actually. I just want you more than anything, Quint, and I really don't care what state the cabin happens to be in."

I came around to her side of the truck, lifted her out with a growl, and carried her to the cabin's door. "I don't want to let you go, but I have to get the key." I slid her down my body, reached up to the ledge above the door, and put the key in the lock.

To my pleasant surprise, it appeared the place had just been cleaned. There were even fresh flowers in a mason jar on the kitchen table.

"Yes, it's just dreadful in here." She came up behind me and put her arms around my waist.

I turned to face her and lifted her so her legs went around my middle. She brought her mouth to mine, and we kissed.

"I'm hearin' you loud and clear, darlin', that you want this just as much as I do, but I gotta ask."

Darrow pulled back and looked into my eyes. "What?"

I dropped my hands and let her slide down my body a second time. I shuddered with the feel of her flush against me and cupped her cheeks with both my hands.

"The reason you came to Texas. How much does the boyfriend play into what's about to happen between us?"

"Ex-boyfriend, and not at all."

"I need you to be sure he doesn't, Darrow, because I don't want you thinking about any other man while you're with me."

"You have no idea how overwhelming you are, Quint. When I'm with you, I can hardly hear my own thoughts. When you walk into a room, it's all I can do not to turn toward you and beg you to take me into your arms. There isn't room for me to think about anyone else, and even if there were, every man I've ever known pales in comparison to you. If you want to know the truth, I've never wanted to be with a man more than I want to be with you right now. And by right now, I mean this second."

With a groan, I lifted her back into my arms, captured her lips, and carried her into the closest bedroom.

"Give me a moment," Darrow said, wiggling out of my arms and sliding down my body a third time. If she continued to do that, I'd lose it before we even gotten naked.

"Where are you running off to?"

"Just to the loo. Don't go anywhere."

I walked the three steps back into the main open-concept room of the cabin with the small kitchen just to the right of the entry. I sat down on the sofa, my gaze resting intently on the bathroom. The moment it reopened, I planned to spring up, get her naked, and on that bed.

Instead, when the door did open, every ounce of air left my lungs. Against the jamb stood Darrow, one hand on her hip. Rather than springing up as planned, I let my gaze move from her intense brown eyes to her blazingly red cheeks, down her long, thin neck, to her heavy breasts with their puckered nipples. Fully dressed, my body reacted to Darrow like I was a teenager who'd never been with a woman before. Seeing her naked in front of me, made me painfully mad with desire.

I took a deep breath, letting my eyes continue down the soft swell of her belly to the hint of her sex that I could barely see since her legs were crossed.

"Open for me," I demanded from where I sat.

Instead of simply uncrossing her legs, Darrow walked toward me until she was close enough to touch. I couldn't resist. I put both hands on her hips and pulled her close enough to breathe in the scent of her. When she started to move, I held her in place.

"Where do you think you're goin', sugar?"

Instead of answering, she took one of my hands in hers and pulled me up off the sofa. "I need you naked too, Quint," she said in the sexiest damn voice I'd ever heard.

Gazing into her eyes, I could see every bit of her uncertainty. She'd been bold in her nakedness, but I could see her beginning to question whether she should've been so daring.

Didn't she know she already owned me? I slid my hands around her waist, cupped both cheeks of her sweet bottom, and pulled her hard against me. "Do you feel what you do to me, Darrow?"

I didn't give her time to answer. Instead, I recaptured her mouth, kissing her softly, slowing things down between us. As much as I wanted to be the one in control, her mouth, her body, everything about her took hold and possessed me. The rhythm of her movement as she gently swayed beneath my touch, tested my patience.

I yanked her closer still, deepened our kiss, and threaded the fingers of one hand into her hair. I thrust my tongue into her mouth roughly, as passion overtook me.

When the vibration of Darrow's moan resonated through me, I raised her leg so her sex rested on my hardness. When she ground against me, I let her.

With my hands fisted in her hair, I pulled her head back so I could feast on the soft skin on her neck. I felt her swallow and lifted her other leg, finally carrying her into the bedroom where I'd vowed to take her what seemed like hours before.

With heat burning brightly between us, I lowered Darrow to the bed and stepped back to let my gaze linger on her spread out before me. When she tried to close her legs, I rested both hands on her knees and gently forced them back open.

"Let me see you, Darrow. All of you." It was clear by the slow gyration of her hips that she liked the way I watched her. "Touch yourself, baby."

She brought one hand up and fondled her breast, squeezing her nipple and moaning. I knelt at the end of the bed, mapping out where I wanted to touch her first and with what part of my body.

I took the hand resting by her hip and brought it to her pussy. I leaned forward and wound my tongue around her fingers, tasting her as she touched herself.

With one hand, I reached behind me, grabbing the condom I'd tucked into my back pocket and setting it on the bed, beside her.

"Quint, please."

"What, baby?"

"You have too many clothes on."

As hard as it was to move my mouth from between her legs, I stood and pulled my shirt over my head with one hand while I unfastened my jeans with the other. I picked up the condom, opened the foil with my teeth, and rolled it on my cock.

I couldn't wait another minute to be inside her. As difficult as it was, I entered her slowly, wanting to remember every moment of feeling her warmth for the first time.

"God, you feel good," I moaned as I slowly buried myself in her wetness. She wrapped her legs around my waist and moved against me. Soon I couldn't hold back any longer. My pace became frenzied as I drove into her. When she arched against me and squeezed me tightly, I lost all control.

14

Darrow

Every muscle in my body had gone limp. I couldn't even lift my arm when Quint rolled me over on my back. He sat up and looked at his phone.

"Do we need to get back?" I asked, having a hard time keeping my eyes open.

"I do, but you can stay here and sleep if you'd rather."

"Not on your life."

"Why not? I like the idea of you being here naked, waiting for me to come back."

I rolled off the other side of the bed. "And take the chance that one of these other women who try to get your attention steals you from me? No way."

Quint grabbed my wrist and pulled me onto his lap. "The last two hours didn't convince you that no other woman on the face of the earth could catch my eye?"

"I'm not taking any chances. I want you all to myself."

I stood and walked back to the lavatory where I'd left my clothes, swaying my hips as I went. I was about to close the door when I stuck my head back out. Quint was smiling.

"Um, what should I wear?"

"What you have on right now would be fine by me."

I smiled back. "Interesting premise, but let's save that for tomorrow night. Jeans or a dress?"

"I'd love to see you in the sweet yellow dress."

"Is there any work I need to do to help you get ready?"

"No, darlin'. I'm ready whenever you are."

I rolled my eyes and came back into the bedroom to grab the dress, a bra, and pants. Quint grabbed my wrist when I walked by, and took the undergarments out of my hand.

"You won't be needing these tonight."

My eyes opened wide. "Do you not remember how short this dress is?"

"I remember exactly how short it is. It'll be up to you to make sure no other cowboys get a glimpse of what's mine tonight."

"Mmm, so caveman of you." I went back into the lavatory and turned on the water for the shower. Moments later, Quint joined me. When he wrapped his arm around my waist and pulled me against him, I knew we wouldn't be leaving for the rodeo anytime soon.

When Quint was reminded exactly how short the yellow dress was, he relented on allowing me to wear pants—or panties as he called them.

He also told me to grab a pair of jeans, a shirt, and some other boots. When I did, he tossed them into a bag, zipped it up, and took it to the truck.

I was headed out after him when I saw he was on his mobile. Instead of interrupting, I looked in the refrigerator to see if there was any food, pleasantly surprised when I found it well stocked. I'd grown accustomed to having a big American breakfast every morning, and knew Quint would be hungry, only because he was always hungry.

The cabin wasn't far from where the rodeo was being held, and when we got back, I saw that the events were already taking place.

Before Quint could come around to open my door, I climbed out. "Go," I told him, sensing Deck's impatience even though all he'd done was tip his hat in my direction.

"Hi," said a woman approaching me. "I'm Kayleigh. Are you here with King-Alexander?"

I smiled and shook the woman's outstretched hand. "I'm Darrow, and yes, I am."

"Team roping is up next if you want to come and watch."

I followed Kayleigh over to the stands. "These are the ranch's seats," she said, pointing. We both sat down.

"Do you know much about team roping?" the woman asked.

"Not really. I mean, I see them roping all day long at the ranch, but I don't know much about the competition."

"Do you work at the ranch?" the woman asked, looking somewhat surprised.

"I guess you could call it that." I laughed. "I try to stay out of Quint's way is probably a better way to put it."

I caught the slightest movement on the woman's face, giving me a clue as to what was really going on. "Have you and Quint been together long?" I asked.

"Oh!" Kayleigh gasped. "Um, aren't you with Quint?"

"I'm a friend of his sister's actually," I told her, only lying a little by omission.

"Well, Quint and I aren't together either. I mean we have been, but it isn't anything serious."

I raised a brow.

"I got the impression at Big Bend that he'd moved on anyway. That's why I thought you two were together."

I heard an announcement over the loudspeaker stating that the roping event was about to start. I looked over behind the shoots and saw Quint looking over at me. When I saw he wasn't smiling, I blew him a kiss and then turned to Kayleigh.

"Would you be a dear and explain to me what's happening?"

The poor girl looked downright puzzled, but finally said she would.

Quint and Decker were the fourth team on the schedule. By the time they got in position on either side of the chute, I knew most of what I should be looking for.

Quint nodded, watched as the steer broke the barrier, and he and Decker exited behind it on horseback.

"He always does that," said Kayleigh when Quint roped the steer's head.

"What's that?" I asked, not turning my head as I watched Decker rope the steer's hind legs. Within what seemed a split second, the steer was tied off and the two men on horseback were in position, facing one another. I looked up at the board and saw a time of 3.7 seconds.

"That's really good," said Kayleigh. "They aren't just the leaders here so far tonight; that's only two-tenths of a second off the world record."

My focus stayed on Quint until the next team got into position and I couldn't see where he'd gone.

"You were going to tell me what he always does," I said, turning to Kayleigh.

"Oh, right. It's hard to explain unless you're watching it. I'll try to show you when the next team goes."

I didn't have to wait long before I saw the next header nod. The steer broke the barrier, and the header threw his rope.

"See right there, how he missed? Well, Quint does that, or he makes everyone think he's missed, and in the last possible millisecond, he flips that rope so precisely that it catches the steer's head. They call it fishing."

"Ah," I said, nodding my head and smiling.

A few minutes later, I saw Quint on his way toward me in the stands.

"Hey, darlin'," he said, leaning down to kiss me. "Hi, Kayleigh."

"Uh, hi, Quint," the other woman said when he put his arm around my shoulders and pulled me close to him.

"Whatcha think? Did Kayleigh here explain it all to you?"

"She did," I said, smiling at the other woman. "She even explained fishing."

Quint's smile broadened. "I told you it would be more interesting if you saw it instead of having me explain it to you."

"Excuse me," they both heard Kayleigh say as she got up and left.

"You wanna tell me what that's all about?" he asked, his smile still stretching across his face.

"She introduced herself and offered to explain team roping to me."

"Huh."

"She also told me that at the Big Bend rodeo, she got the impression you weren't interested in her anymore."

"Listen, we were just—"

"Before you say another word, know that if you tell me anything whatsoever about Kayleigh, you will be forced to listen to the same details about Axel."

"Axel? That's his name?"

I nodded. "Although many people, my brothers included, call him Pinch."

"Stop right there. I don't want to hear another word, and we can also forget talking about ol' what's her name."

Quint leaned forward and kissed me, which I deepened.

"Mmm, what's that for?" he asked, pulling back just slightly. "Not that I'm complaining."

"Two-tenths of a second off the world record."

15

Quint

I took a lot of ribbing from the other cowboys, but I didn't care. I'd never had so much fun at a ranch rodeo, and it was all because of Darrow. Looking at things through her curious eyes, made everything feel new to me again.

The fact that she picked up on the things I told her so quickly made it challenging to keep up. Some of the questions she asked were about details I'd never thought about before.

All too soon, it was time for us to go home, and when we got there, I had no idea what to expect, and guessed she didn't either.

We'd spent the last two nights in each other's arms, albeit without much rest. I wasn't one to stay in a woman's bed after sex, so I wasn't sure how well I'd sleep anyway. By the time we finished pounding as much pleasure as we could out of each other's bodies, we'd both fallen asleep out of sheer exhaustion.

We were an hour out from the ranch when I broached the subject. "The bed in the room you're staying in is bigger than mine."

She lifted her head from my shoulder and smiled. "Are you *fishing* for an invitation, cowboy?"

I laughed. She'd managed to work that word in wherever she could at least a dozen times.

"Sure as sugar am, sugar."

"Consider the invitation open, then."

She put her head back on my shoulder, and I squeezed her thigh.

"What's wrong, Darrow? You tensed up."

"Perhaps we should take Wren's feelings into consideration before our sleeping in the same bed becomes a foregone conclusion."

I looked out the driver's side window. Darrow was right, but I couldn't imagine having that conversation with my sister. I hoped Darrow wouldn't mind handling it.

When we went inside, Wren was nowhere to be found. I walked through the house, calling her name. When I got to the last room, what had been our mother's library, I saw her asleep in a chair.

"Where is she?" Darrow asked from behind me.

"In here," I answered, switching on the lights.

Wren covered her eyes.

"What are you doing in here?" I asked.

"I must've dozed off, looking at pictures."

Darrow walked over and picked up the photo album that had fallen to the floor. "Oh my goodness," she gasped, setting the heavy leather book on a table. "That's my mother and father."

"Seriously?" I said, looking over Darrow's shoulder.

"Look, Wren," she said, pointing.

"I didn't realize Z knew the duke," my sister answered, looking over Darrow's other shoulder.

"Of course he did. My father was the one who helped Z get the job with SIS."

I watched as Wren's eyes met Darrow's and my sister covered her mouth to stifle a gasp.

Seconds later, Wren left the room.

"Who is that?" Quint asked.

"That's my father, although in this photo, he looks just like my brother Sutton."

"Maybe you should talk to her," I suggested.

"I will." Darrow stood on tiptoes and kissed me. "Thank you so much for a wonderful weekend, and thanks for not turning into Ebenezer Scrooge on the drive home."

I smiled, smacked her bottom when she walked away to find Wren, and studied the photo album sitting on the table. My father looked so young in the pictures, but my mother didn't look much different than the way I remembered her. Not that I remembered much. Wren and I were so young when she died. I often wondered if she remembered our mom at all.

I couldn't imagine being in my father's shoes when it happened. Not only did he have to care for his beloved wife as a horrific disease spread through her body, but he had two young children to watch over at the same time. Tee-Tee had stepped in to help as much as she could, but I remembered wishing so much that it was my mother reading me a story before bedtime instead of the woman with the thick Hispanic accent.

When I looked back on it now, I realized we would've all been lost without her.

Z was only twenty-eight years old when his wife and mother of his children had died, three years younger than I was now. I couldn't imagine dealing with a loss like my dad had. I hardly knew Darrow, yet if she became ill with a terminal disease, I'd be devastated.

Darrow found me later, still thumbing through the photo albums.

"Tell me about her."

"I don't remember much. Little things."

"Like?"

"Her voice more than anything else. She always spoke so softly. She was a real lady."

"My mother is like that. I know my brothers wish I was more like her."

I pulled her to sit on my lap. "I like you just the way you are, Darrow."

"You haven't known me that long."

"That's the second time you've said something to that effect, and it bothers me."

"See? You're finding things already."

I frowned. "That isn't what I said."

The smile left her face, and she tried to get up from my lap, but I wouldn't let her.

"I like you just the way you are, Darrow," I repeated.

"Thank you, Quint."

"See? Was that so hard?"

She rolled her eyes and tried a second time to get up. "Where am I sleeping tonight, sugar?"

"With me?"

"I wasn't sure the timing was right for you to discuss it with Wren."

"Discuss it with Wren? We're adults, Quint. I can't quite imagine how a conversation so ridiculous would go. Are you truly thinking we need your sister's permission?"

I shrugged. "I guess not."

"Come on, cowboy, let's go to bed."

16

Darrow

"I love that place," I said when Quint and I were on the drive home from the Long Branch. I'd learned not to order my own meal, instead getting Quint to share his, although tonight he brought some home with him.

"Gotta save room for Thanksgiving dinner," he said when I'd expressed surprise at his diminished appetite.

"It's my first Thanksgiving." I was so excited. There were people in England who celebrated it, my family included, but I doubted it was anything as authentic as what they did in the States.

"It'll be different this year with Wren home and you with us. In years past, all the cowboys would gather in the bunkhouse and eat cafeteria-style. Then again, everything is different, having you here." Quint leaned forward and kissed me before helping me out of the truck.

The last two months had been a dream. Between my relationship with Quint and my friendship with Wren,

I'd never known such happiness. Every day, I looked forward to the new things I'd learn and experience. Most days, I rode out with Wren, but at some point, we'd meet up with Quint and I would spend the rest of the day with him.

"When you're with Wren, I miss havin' my pretty little shadow followin' behind me."

He said it so often that that's what he started calling me, and I loved it.

Soon it would be Christmas, the first I spent away from the UK. Part of me felt guilty for not wanting to spend it with my family, although there were plenty of holidays where either one or both of my brothers had begged off.

We walked inside, arm in arm, chatting and laughing until we saw Wren doubled over at the bar in the kitchen, sobbing.

"Wren, what's happened?" I asked, racing over to her with Quint right on my heels.

"Is it Z?" he asked.

Wren shook her head.

"Please, Wren. Tell us," said her brother.

"It was Wilder," she said between sobs.

I covered my mouth. "What's happened?"

"It's Wellie."

"Oh, God, no. Not Wellie." I grabbed the back of the barstool, almost doubling over myself.

I was so selfish, so thoughtless. I'd just been thinking about how happy I was that I wasn't going back to England for the holidays, and now the man who was like a second father to me was gone, and I hadn't talked to him in weeks.

The pain of losing Wellie was the worst I'd felt since my father died.

"I'm so sorry to worry you this way," Wren said, standing to put her hand on my shoulder. "He's ill, and Wilder has asked that you please come home as soon as possible."

Quint took me in his arms, and I rested my head on his chest.

"I have to go to him."

"Of course you do."

"I'm so sorry, Quint."

He leaned away and cupped my cheek. "There's nothing for you to be sorry for. I only wish I could go with you, but I can't, sweetheart."

"Why can't you?"

"God, I feel terrible, but it's fall calving season. We're at risk of losing too many calves if cold weather kicks in as it is. Without me here, I can't fathom how bad it could get."

"It's okay. I'm going home. I'll be fine." I wiped at my tears. Again, I was thinking of myself when the only person who I should be considering was Wellie.

The next morning, Quint drove Wren and me to the airport. I'd told them both that it wasn't necessary for Wren to go with me, but neither would relent.

I'd spent much of the last few hours crying and didn't have it in me to argue.

It was harder than I imagined it would be to say goodbye to Quint. I wished I could beg him to come with me, but I couldn't. Again, that would be so incredibly selfish. He had a ranch to run.

"Call me as soon as you can," Quint said, kissing me goodbye. "If you have to stay, I'll come as soon as it looks like Deck and the crew can handle the calves on their own."

I clung to him. It was silly, but somewhere deep inside, it felt like I'd never see him again.

He kissed me one last time when Wren said we needed to get to the plane, and then he was gone.

Once through security, Wren excused herself to make a phone call.

"Who was that?" I asked when Wren rejoined me. "Was that Sutton?"

"No, sweetheart. I was calling Z."

"Why?"

"He's going to meet us at the airport."

"Why?" I asked again.

Wren put her hand on the small of my back, navigating me toward the flight attendant who was asking for all first-class passengers to board.

"He's going to give us a lift to the abbey."

"But Sutton is picking us up. I spoke to him just after Quint purchased the tickets."

Wren looked upset by my news. Had I done the wrong thing by calling him?

Once we were seated, I closed my eyes. I was physically and mentally exhausted.

"Wake up, sweetie," I heard Wren say. "We're getting ready to land."

I sat up and looked at my watch. "Already? Did I really sleep the entire flight?"

"You did."

I looked out the window at the dreary London weather. If someone had told me forty-eight hours ago that I'd be going home, I would've laughed at them first and then prayed they were wrong. There was next to nothing that would bring me here, outside of the health of someone I loved.

Wren helped me navigate to customs. Thankfully, with her credentials and the diplomat passport I carried because of my family, we were ushered through quickly. I looked at the faces in the crowd for Sutton, but didn't see him. Instead, I saw Axel.

He looked in such pain that I prayed I wasn't too late. As soon as they let me, I ran into his arms.

"How is he?"

"He's hanging on. He can't wait to see you." When Axel leaned forward to kiss me, I turned my cheek.

"Where is Wren?"

Axel motioned across the walkway to where my friend stood talking to my brother.

"Come on, let's get your trunk," Axel said, guiding me away from where Wren and Sutton stood.

"I need to wait for her."

"Wilder drove also; he'll bring her to the abbey."

I wished I could confirm that with Wren, but she and Sutton looked deep in conversation. Finally, I relented and let Axel lead me away.

"I missed you so much, Darrow," he said, taking my hand and bringing it to his lips.

"Axel, we need to talk."

"And we shall. Let's get you back to the abbey so you can see Wellie, then you and I can talk this out."

I inwardly groaned. As far as I was concerned, we had nothing to "talk out." Axel obviously saw things differently. As soon as we arrived at the abbey, I'd excuse myself somehow and call Quint. I couldn't wait to hear his voice.

17

Quint

What only yesterday promised to be the best Thanksgiving I'd had in years, or maybe ever, turned right back into the same holiday routine I'd experienced for the last ten, at least.

I was sitting in the bunkhouse with the rest of the men and women who lived and worked on the King-Alexander Ranch when an emergency weather alert popped up on my phone. I read it and looked up at Decker, who must've received the same alert. We stood and walked toward each other.

"What the hell does this mean?" Deck asked, going on to read the alert. "'An extra-tropical cyclone is developing ahead of an upper-level trough over the West Coast. Snow is expected to fall as far south as the United States-Mexico border beginning as early as midnight.'"

"It sounds like we're about to get one helluva snowstorm," said one of the other ranch hands.

Decker let out a whistle, and the bunkhouse dining room went silent. "A freak storm is headed our way. We need everyone out that can get out, either on ATV, horse-back, or SUV. We have cattle out, roaming the ranch, some of whom are about to drop calves on the ground."

Lines formed with men taking their dishes to the bins near the kitchen.

"Tell them to just go," yelled Tee-Tee, waving her hands at me. I got Deck's attention.

"Tee-Tee says leave your dishes," Deck yelled out.

I made my way to the back of the barn and threw open one of the alley doors.

"You gettin' out the Bummer?" asked Deck.

"This sounds bad."

Deck nodded and started moving the boxes that were stored around the vehicle he and I had built ourselves. It was what was known as a Frankenstein car, although it was more of a truck. We'd pieced it together from parts of countless others. Once it was assembled, Deck had found buckets of bright-yellow texture paint, and that's what we'd used to paint it. It had all-wheel drive, was lifted higher than any of our other trucks, and the tires were from an abandoned military vehicle.

I got in, praying it would start, and it did on the first try. "What the hell do you know!"

"I start it up about once a week," said Deck, climbing in the passenger side.

We weren't a mile out when heavy winds started picking up. Somewhere off in the distance, I could swear I heard tornado sirens going off. "Were tornadoes predicted?" I asked. Deck looked at his phone.

"Fuck!" he shouted, reading something on his screen.

"Tell me what the hell is goin' on, Deck!"

"It says tornadic supercells have begun to appear in areas of Texas. One cell is reported to have produced an EF4 wedge. More are expected."

"That comes through here, and there won't be anything left."

Within the hour, heavy wind and rain that turned into blizzard-like snow descended on the ranch. I couldn't see a foot in front of me. I told Deck to get on the radio and tell everyone who was out to get the hell back to the main buildings. We'd lose a lot of cattle tonight, but I didn't intend to lose the lives of our ranch hands.

"Power's out," Deck reported. "One of the guys is headed back to make sure the generators kick on."

Things were going from bad to worse. I had no idea what to expect by light of the next day, but I knew it would be far worse than I could even imagine.

Deck and I, along with the rest of the men who were out in vehicles, stayed out all night and into the following day. Most of the cattle we came upon were already gone. Every so often, we'd find one or two alive. If they'd already dropped their calves, they were dead too.

With over a hundred thousand acres, it would take days for us to cover all the ground. I'd stopped worrying about my cell phone hours ago. Everyone was relying on radio communication instead, and it was important to keep that equipment charged.

Forty-eight hours after I got the first weather alert, Deck convinced me that I needed to sleep. I stumbled into the ranch house and into the bed I'd shared with Darrow. That seemed like weeks ago, given all I'd been through and seen.

I had no estimate of how many head of cattle we'd lost, but I knew it would be numbered in the thousands. We wouldn't be alone in this, either. Every ranch in the region had to have experienced the same devastating losses.

I hugged the pillow that still smelled like Darrow and fell into a deep but troubled sleep.

18

Darrow

I suffered through a miserable Thanksgiving dinner prepared by the Whittaker family cook, Mrs. Mollybock. She made no secret throughout the meal service that she was very put out that Sutton wasn't there.

"She loves him and hates me," Thornton grumbled.

"Why is that?" I asked. "She's never acted this way toward me."

"It's me. All me. I have no idea why, but she's never liked me."

I would have at least tried to assuage my oldest brother's hurt feelings, but it was pointless. Mrs. Mollybock glared in his direction every time she came into the room.

The only other person Mrs. Mollybock seemed to be concerned about was Wellie, and for that, I wouldn't complain. He was home now and telling everyone he was feeling better although he certainly wasn't up for joining us for a formal dinner at the abbey.

I promised Axel I'd leave as soon as I was able and bring them both leftovers from the meal. When I arrived, I saw that the cook had beat me to it. Evidently, she'd prepared a meal solely for them.

On my way to Wellie's cottage, I'd tried to call Quint. I'd been trying for the last twenty-four hours, and my calls went straight to his voicemail. The same thing happened when I tried to contact Wren.

"I'm sorry I haven't had much time to talk," Axel said when he came out of his father's bedchamber.

"It's okay. Wellie's health should be our primary concern."

When he reached for me, I turned away.

"What's going on?" he asked, leading me away from the door and into the sitting room.

"We broke up, Axel. I went to America. Have you somehow forgotten?"

"You're back now, and I thought we could—"

"We can't," I answered more abruptly than I intended.

He pulled me over to the sofa. "I'm listening, Darrow. Tell me what's happened in the time since you left the abbey."

"I can't do this right now, Axel. I'll go in to see your father, and then I need to get back to the abbey."

When I peeked in, Wellie was sound asleep.

"I'll come back in the morning."

"Right," he said, hands in his pockets. "Tell me this. Is there someone else?"

Was there? I didn't know what to think. Why would Quint leave his mobile off for hours on end? Had he invited the pretty cowgirl to join him for Thanksgiving dinner? What was her name? Kayleigh?

No. Of course he wouldn't do that, but what logical explanation could there be? He'd told me to ring him when I arrived in London, and I had. Repeatedly.

"Darrow?"

"I'm sorry, Axel. There is, or at least there was, someone else. But that is really beside the point. We broke up. When I went to America, our relationship was over."

"I'd hoped that once you were back, we could…I don't know…try again."

"To what end? If you recall, this last breakup was your idea. We aren't suited, Axel. You know this as well as I do. Perhaps better. I don't know where your idea of a reconciliation came from."

"I missed you."

"I missed you too, but that isn't a reason to continually perpetuate a relationship that doesn't work for either of us. I'll say it again, I'm sorry, but I've got to go."

Three days later, I was at my wit's end. I still hadn't been able to reach Quint or Wren. Finally I called Sutton.

"I promise, by noon. No later," Sutton said when I pressed him on when they'd be arriving at the abbey.

"Is Wren nearby? May I speak with her?"

"Yes, she's right here," Sutton answered.

"Hello, Darrow."

I couldn't begin to explain how good it felt to hear my friend's voice. "I thought perhaps the two of you had been swallowed by a black hole. You missed Thanksgiving."

Wren laughed. "We flew through Thanksgiving, and you slept the entire time."

"Mrs. Mollybock made quite a feast followed by an equally dramatic fuss when her precious Sutton didn't arrive for dinner. You do know he's her favorite."

"Mrs. Mollybock?"

I heard Sutton groan in the background.

"The cook. There's only two people she gives a wit about, Sutton and Wellie. The rest of us could eat porridge morning, noon, and night for all she cares."

"Speaking of Wellie, how is he doing?"

"Much better, thank God."

"I can't wait to meet him."

"I keep forgetting you haven't. You must hurry and get up here. Tell Sutton he's not allowed to hold you hostage any longer."

"I will. We're leaving soon. I promise. Oh, and I may need to borrow some clothes."

I laughed. "Right, of course. Um, Wren, I have a question."

"Go ahead."

"Wait, hang on one minute." I didn't want anyone to overhear this part of our conversation. "Okay, I've gone outside. Have you spoken to Quint?"

"I haven't. To be honest, I haven't spoken to anyone other than your brother. Why?"

"I was just wondering. We'll talk more when you get here. Do hurry."

I rang off and tried Quint's mobile again. I'd lost count of how many times I had.

When I returned to the abbey, I found Orina, Thornton's wife, in the sitting room.

"Come talk with me, Darrow," she said, holding out her hand.

I sat on the sofa next to her and fell against its back.

"Tell me what's troubling you."

"Are you sure you want to know?"

Orina covered my hand with hers. "You're like a sister to me. So yes, I want to know. You haven't been yourself since you returned from America. I know you were concerned about Wellie, but I sense there's something more."

Tears streamed down my cheeks as I told my brother's wife everything that had happened between Quint Alexander and me, including that I hadn't been able to reach him since I arrived in England.

"There has to be an explanation. Have you asked Wren?"

"Of course I have, but only when I called Sutton earlier. Prior to that, I couldn't reach her either."

Orina bit her bottom lip. "I can see how that would be upsetting. We'll press her for more information when she and Wilder arrive."

When my sister-in-law brushed the hair from my face and cupped my cheek, I started crying all over again.

"Thank you."

"Come here." Orina pulled me closer and put her arm around my shoulders. "If you need to cry, cry."

I smiled. It was rare that one heard even the tiniest bit of Orina's Russian accent, but I had then. It usually came out when she was either angry or sad. I guessed this time it was because Orina felt sorry for me.

"I have a story to tell you."

I wiped my tears. "Okay."

"As you are well aware, when I realized I was pregnant, I kept that information from your brother. In fact, I went into hiding, from him and everyone else."

"You were in danger, Orina. United Russia had a bounty on your head."

"This is true, but there was more to it. I wasn't sure about a relationship with Shiver—Thornton, as you call him. We were from such different worlds. I grew up an orphan in Moscow, and he was the eldest son of a duke."

"That didn't matter to him, Orina. He loved you."

My sister-in-law smiled. "I know that now, and I supposed I did then too, but there's something more I want you to know."

"Go on. I'm sorry I keep interrupting."

"When Kazmir was born, I thought a lot about our relationship. I focused entirely on Shiver as my son's father rather than the man I loved. For some reason, I thought the two were mutually exclusive. Those first few months of my son's life, I learned so much about myself. Having a baby…there is a lot of time to think. I realized that Kazmir and I would be okay on our own."

"I'm so glad it didn't work out that way. For both your sakes. Or all three of yours. And now, Lilliya's too."

"When we found our way back to each other, it was so different. Instead of needing Shiver in my life, I wanted him. Do you understand the difference, Darrow?"

"I think so."

"It may sound silly, but I made friends with myself in those early months of my son's life. I knew who I was, and I learned to like 'me.' The life I led before he was born…I wasn't a good person, Darrow. I'll spare you the details, but it wasn't easy to look at myself in the mirror. That's the expression, right?"

I smiled. "Yes, that's right."

"I don't know if I'm making sense to you, but what I'm trying to say is, don't skip that part. Get to know yourself, learn to be okay with yourself. You don't need to be in a relationship to be complete."

I blinked away my tears. Orina had spoken directly to my every insecurity. Who was I if not the daughter of one duke and duchess, sister of another, and someone's girlfriend? On my own, I had nothing. It was the reason I'd left England in the first place. I'd gone to America to figure out what I wanted to do with the rest of my life and, instead, immediately got into a relationship with Wren's brother. I didn't do anything to forge my own life; I became part of his.

Perhaps it was for the best that I hadn't heard from Quint. That was what Orina was telling me, wasn't it? Being okay on my own was a tall order, but maybe being forced to come back to England was for the best too. I'd had my talk with Axel, and while he didn't agree at the time, deep down he knew we didn't belong together. It was as much a convenience for him as it was for me.

So here I was on my own with nothing to do but get to know myself—something I would've gladly avoided doing if not for my sister-in-law's lecture. I wasn't a child, though. It was time I grew up and took responsibility for my own life and what I did with it.

"I think they've arrived," said Orina.

I stood, looked at my watch, and peered out the window. Had an hour gone by already? "The duchess is here as well. Wait. You're the duchess. Let me rephrase. My mother is here, as is Sir Caird."

Orina nodded, seemingly completely unaffected by the crowd of people arriving at the abbey.

"I wish I could be as calm as you are."

"Oh, Darrow." She laughed. "Inside, I am a barrel of jumping monkeys."

That wasn't an analogy I'd ever heard in regard to being anxious; however, I knew what Orina meant.

I waited until I couldn't stand it anymore and ran from the sitting room to the vestibule.

"Is that Wren?" I shouted.

Sutton cleared his throat.

"What?" I looked at him with hands on my hips.

"I've not seen you since summer."

"Oh, sorry." I hastily kissed both of his cheeks before grabbing Wren's hand and pulling her back to the sitting room.

"Tell me what's happened between you and Sutton."

"I wouldn't know where to begin," said Wren, leaning over to kiss Orina's cheek. "It's good to see you, Losha."

Orina stood, and she and Wren hugged. "You look happy."

"Very much so, in fact."

Wren sat down between us and gave a brief rundown of what had happened between her and Sutton over the course of the last few days.

"It took a while, but we both finally admitted our real feelings. Well, it took me longer than it took your brother."

"What does that mean?"

"It means…" Wren's mobile vibrated, and she looked at the screen. I couldn't help myself; I looked too and was disappointed to see the name Vera rather than Quint. "I'm sorry. I need to take this."

Wren left the room, and I felt my face fall. I hadn't had the chance to even ask her about Quint.

"Come with me," said Orina. "Your niece and nephew have missed you."

"I'm a terrible aunt. I haven't even asked about them today. Is Kazmir feeling better?"

"Yes, I think so," said Orina. "Too much of that ghastly pie. What was it? Pumpkin?" She shuddered and I laughed.

Orina was right, what I needed more than anything was a strong dose of unconditional love, and I knew just where to get it.

19

Quint

I rested my head in my hands. Based on the counts we'd received, King-Alexander Ranch lost over ten thousand head of cattle in the storm. Numbers were coming in from all over; the devastation was felt state-wide and throughout the Midwest. The cattle industry would be impacted by the losses for decades.

I needed to talk to both my father and sister, but I couldn't bring myself to place the call. When I did, I'd be forced to tell them how badly I'd failed.

It didn't matter how many pep talks Tee-Tee tried to give me; the bottom line was, I was a steward of the land and the livestock. It was my job to protect both, and I hadn't.

"It could've been a lot worse," said Deck. "We saved three-quarters of the herd. You have to look at it that way, Quint."

I stared at my phone and all the missed calls from Darrow. I needed to call her too, but every time I thought about it, it was either too late in England, or Deck came to me with yet another emergency to be handled.

I missed her so much, I ached. It was a different kind of ache than the ones that had settled in my body and mind. This was an ache in my heart.

I needed to hear her voice, but was that fair of me? She was there because someone important to her was dying. Could I really dump my problems on her in the face of that?

I set down the phone I'd just picked up.

"You need to call her," said Deck, standing to leave the room.

"I can't."

My friend left, shaking his head as he walked away.

20

Darrow

I had no idea what had transpired between the time when I went to the nursery with Orina and when my mother came in and woke me.

"Hello, sweetheart," she whispered.

I sat up and looked around. Both Kazmir and Lilliya were sound asleep as I'd been. "What time is it?"

"Just after six. I've been sent to fetch you for dinner."

"Dinner? At this hour?" The Whittakers never had dinner before eight o'clock.

"Yes, well, there seems to be a guest from the States, although I don't know why that should matter, but anyway, it is what it is, Darrow. Come and join us."

I stood, stretched my stiff muscles, and hugged her. "Are you happy, Mother?"

"Yes, sweetheart. I'm happy. Are you?"

I linked our arms. "Not so much."

"I'm sorry to hear that. What can I do to help?"

"Nothing, I fear," I sighed.

When we arrived in the dining room, there were two places empty. One was next to Sir Caird and the other next to Axel.

I took my seat, folded my hands, and settled into irrelevance.

"Darrow?" said Wren from across the table. "A walk between courses?"

"Yes. I'd love it," I answered. I'd been sitting in relative silence for over a half hour and was just about to get up and leave as it was.

"Thank you," I whispered, following Wren into the entryway where we grabbed our overcoats.

We'd just gotten outside when I saw the woman who had been seated on the other side of Axel come out the front door as well.

"I owe you an apology," said the woman who I thought had been introduced as Vera. "I was monopolizing the conversation."

"It's all right," I responded without adding how used to it I was.

"It isn't. It was rude."

I knew it was rude, but I didn't say anything more. I really didn't care at this point. All I wanted to do was go and visit Wellie before retreating to my own bed-chamber in Covington House for the rest of the night.

"What's wrong?" Wren asked once the woman had gone back inside. "How are things with you and Pinch?"

"It isn't the same as it used to be between us. We're barely friends."

"Could it get better?"

"It could, but it hasn't."

"Darrow, I hope my brother doesn't play into this in any way. Quint isn't exactly…"

"What? Finish what you were going to say about him."

"He isn't the relationship type."

I raised a brow. "I've never met someone who treats a woman the way your brother does. He's a gentleman. Your brother would never leave me sitting there while he spent the entire dinner talking to the woman seated on the other side of him."

"I don't know what to say about that."

"The thing between Axel and me has run its course."

"You don't know; it might still work out."

I stopped walking. "I'm not interested in it working out, and I don't believe he is either. Wren, are you opposed to my relationship with your brother?"

Wren stopped too. "I'm not. However, I was there when we got off the plane, and you were quite happy to see Axel. I have to admit I was glad Quint wasn't there to see it."

Wren had it wrong. While I may have run to him, it was only out of concern for Wellie. "We've known each other since we were children. Sometimes it's more like he's my brother."

"And sometimes it's not."

That wasn't true anymore, but I wasn't interested in arguing with Wren. I'd believed her to be an ally, but I was quickly coming to realize she wasn't anything of the sort.

"I was the only person at the table who had no clue what everyone else was talking about. Even my mother understood what was going on."

"It's difficult when everyone else is talking shop. I'll be mindful we don't do so much of that when we go back in."

"I've a headache anyway. I'll visit with Wellie before I go back to Covington House."

"I wish you would come back inside with me instead."

"Remember when I told you I never wanted to come back to England?"

Wren nodded.

"I had my reasons."

I let myself into Wellie's cottage as quietly as I could. If I found him sleeping, I'd leave and come back tomorrow.

Instead, when the door creaked open, I saw him sitting in his chair by the fire, talking to Mrs. Mollybock.

"Look who's here," the woman said, jumping up. "'Tis the bairn, Darrow. Come here, my sweet."

Miss Molly, as I'd called her when I was a little girl, seemed in a far better mood than she'd been at Thanksgiving. I supposed that had much to do with Sutton's return earlier today.

"We've had our visit. I'll be heading back to the abbey, then."

"You don't have to leave on my account," I told her, walking over to kiss Wellie's cheek.

"Mr. Fulton was just commenting that he hadn't had a chance to speak to you on his own, isn't that right?"

I looked between the two people who had played such a significant role in my childhood, and smiled when Wellie winked at me.

"Good evening, Mrs. Mollybock," he said when she left through the kitchen door. "Come and sit with me, Darrow."

"Are you sure you're up for a visit? I can come back in the morning."

"Sit, lass. I've missed you so."

My eyes filled with tears when I sat on the floor beside him. "I'm so sorry."

He reached out and stroked my hair, making me cry all the more.

"Tell me, how was your American adventure?"

"I wish I'd come back sooner, but only to see you. The rest I could do without. I'm back to being invisible."

"You are the only one who sees yourself that way, Darrow. To everyone else, you light up the room."

"You're always so sweet to me, Wellie, but I am far less illuminating than you've always believed."

"Tell me what's happened."

"To begin, you know that Axel and I are finished, right?"

"I am more aware of that fact than he is, I fear."

"Yes. Well, that's my fault. Although we talked earlier. I reminded him that he ended things between us before I left. Not the other way around."

"Better that you talked it out."

"I know," I said, resting my head against Wellie's knee. "What would I do without you? I was terrified when I thought I was about to find out."

"There's still lots of life left in this old bugger."

"I'm so glad, Wellie. Truly. You do know how much you mean to me?"

"Yes, lass," he said, stroking my hair. "You're like my own."

"Are you terribly disappointed about Axel and me?"

"Not at all. You will both find the lives you are supposed to live, even if it's without each other."

I sighed. "You never thought it was a good idea."

Wellie laughed. "Don't put words in my mouth, lass. Now be a dear and fetch us both a brandy."

"Are you allowed?"

"If I'm not, I'd sooner die."

I stood and shook my finger at him. "Don't say that."

I pulled the unmarked bottle from the shelf in the kitchen and poured two glasses. Knowing he'd likely want more, I brought the bottle with me and set it on the table next to him. Instead of sitting on the floor, I sat in the chair.

Wellie leveled his gaze at me. "There's more you haven't told me."

"I don't know there's much more to tell. I mean there was when I left America, but since I arrived in England, I'm uncertain."

"Start at the beginning, lass."

I told Wellie everything from the time I went to Z and begged him to let me know where Wren was, all the way through getting on the plane in Texas, of course leaving out the part about my intimacy with Quint.

"Have you not seen the news, Darrow?" he asked, sitting forward in his chair. "Turn the telly on."

"What are you about, Wellie?"

"Do as I ask, lass."

I picked up the remote that sat near his chair and turned the power on. I handed it to him to find the station he wanted to watch.

"It's been on, near nonstop. The news out of the States is devastating, Darrow."

"In what way? What's happened?"

"Thanksgiving night, a terrible storm went through. Tornadoes, snowstorms. It was a bloody mess. It still is."

I pulled my mobile out of my pocket and rang Wren, praying she'd answer even though they were likely still gathered in the dining room. As I expected, my friend did not pick up.

Next I tried the abbey's main line.

"Whittaker Abbey," answered Mrs. Mollybock.

"Thank God. Miss Molly, I need you to fetch Wren. It's urgent that I speak with her."

I heard the phone drop on the counter.

"You can up the volume," I told Wellie, who had turned it down when I made my first call.

While I waited for Wren to come to the phone, I watched the news report. Hundreds of thousands of cattle were reported dead already, although the numbers were expected to increase.

The winter storm, which reached epic proportions, didn't hit Texas alone; it ravaged most of the country. The East Coast was currently undergoing blizzard conditions. Power was out, people were stranded, deaths were being reported.

"What is it, Darrow?" asked Wren, sounding breathless.

"A freak storm hit Texas the day we left. It's bad, Wren. We need to try to reach Quint. If not him, someone who can tell us the state of things at the ranch." And someone who could tell us if Quint was okay, but I didn't say that part.

"I haven't heard a thing about this," she mumbled.

"Me either. I rarely watch the telly as it is…Wellie is the one who saw the reports."

"I need to try to reach Quint."

"Yes. Please let me know as soon as you've heard."

"Of course." Wren ended the call.

21

Quint

My sister beat me to the punch; my cell was ringing, and Wren's name appeared on the screen. It was only two in the afternoon, but I didn't care. I poured myself a fourth shot of whiskey and downed it before I accepted the call.

"Hello, Wren."

"Quint, I've just been talking to Darrow. None of us had seen the news. Wellie did, probably because he was in hospital. What in God's name is happening?"

I'd anticipated that this conversation would be one of the hardest of my life, but faced with it, it was even more difficult than I'd expected.

"We lost a lot…of cattle, Wren." My voice cracked mid-sentence.

"What about you? What about the rest of the ranch hands? Tee-Tee? Decker? Are they all okay?"

"We're all fine. The tornadoes went all around us. It was the blizzard that did us in."

"Tornadoes? God, Darrow wasn't specific, her main concern was that I reach you as soon as possible. She's been calling you relentlessly, Quint."

"This is the first I've been in the house to do more than fall down, dead tired. Every time I thought about calling…" I stopped talking. I didn't need to explain myself. I hadn't answered or called back, because I couldn't. I was too busy trying to save my cattle and my ranch. "Look, I don't want to get into that right now. My next call was to be to you and Z. Do you know where he is?"

"He's here at Whittaker Abbey. We all are."

"Can you get him? It'll be easier if I can tell you both at once."

"Of course, I'm walking to the dining room now."

I waited, scrubbing my face with my hand. I needed to talk to Darrow. I wanted to, but this conversation had to come first.

I could hear my sister telling our father that I was on the phone and that they needed to go somewhere quiet.

"Okay, Quint, we're both here. I'm going to put you on speaker now."

"Hey, Z. I'm afraid the news isn't good."

"Go ahead, son. Tell us."

"We lost twenty-five percent of the herd, at least. Close to one hundred percent of the fall calves. We don't have our final counts yet."

"God, Quint, I'm so sorry."

I had tears in my eyes and was too choked up to speak. If I did, they'd know I hadn't just failed to protect my herd, but I wasn't man enough to control my emotions.

"I'll be on the next flight," said Z. "Whatever we need to do, we'll do together."

"There's no point. Every day we're burying more and more of our herd. You don't want to come here and see this."

"That isn't why I'd come. I'd come for you, son. I'm not taking no for an answer."

"I'm sorry I didn't return right away, Quint," said Wren.

"I appreciate that, but there wasn't anything you could've done. You only would've been putting yourself in danger."

"Quint, what should I tell Darrow?"

"She isn't there?"

"No. She was with Wellie. He's the one who saw the news reports. I think I may have already told you. Of course she wants me to call her back as soon as we're finished talking."

"Don't. Let me call her myself."

"Will you? She's beyond frantic."

"The minute we hang up. I promise."

"Z, is there anything else?" I heard Wren ask.

"Call Darrow. If I think of anything, I'll call you when I get to the airport."

"I think Vera is leaving shortly. You could ride back with her," Wren said to our father. "Sorry, Quint. I'll let you go."

"I'll be in touch, Wren."

She disconnected the call on her end, and I stared at my phone. I needed to get this over with. Once I told Darrow about the loss of so many of the herd, I hoped I didn't have to tell anyone else.

"Quint?"

"Hello, darlin'," I said when she answered my call. I hadn't even heard her phone ring on my end.

"I've been so worried."

"I know and I'm sorry. Things have been pretty rough around here."

"I saw the news reports. I'm so sorry, Quint."

Should I tell her how bad it really was for us? Would she want to know? I had no idea how to handle this situation. The last time I'd had a woman in my life even semi-permanently, I was in college. Or was it high school?

"Quint, are you still there?"

"Yeah, I'm here."

"I miss you so much."

I could hear the emotion in her voice. "I miss you too, Darrow. I haven't had time to even think, but when I do, you're on my mind." *You're on my mind? Jesus.* I really didn't do this phone thing well at all. "How is Wellie?"

"He seems better. He's home. He was the one who told me about, you know, the weather."

"Glad to hear he's better."

"He isn't out of the woods yet. I'm…um…I know you didn't ask, but…I think I should stay on here longer."

"You have to do what you think is best, Darrow."

"Okay. Well, thanks for calling, Quint."

"Sure. You take care now."

22

Darrow

I came back into the sitting room of Wellie's cottage. Trying my hardest to hold off my tears until I could say good night to him. If I didn't, it would be the second time I cried on the man's shoulder over the span of an hour.

"Come over here, lass."

"I've really got to go, Wellie. I'll come back in the morning."

"No, you aren't going anywhere until you tell me why you're about to cry."

I really should've known better than to think Wellie wouldn't pick up on how I was feeling. He always had. In so many ways he'd been more like a father to me than the duke was. I loved him, but Wellie...he loved me.

Instead of sitting in a chair, I sat on the floor next to him, rested my head on his knee, and cried.

"There, there," he said, stroking my hair. "Cry it out, lass. Cry it out."

"It was like we were strangers."

Wellie didn't say anything. I knew he was waiting for me to, but I didn't know how to respond. I didn't know how I felt, so how could I explain it to him? The conversation was so bloody awkward. Was he just so exhausted from his ordeal? He said he hadn't had time to think.

Orina's words from earlier echoed in my head. I'd decided then it was for the best that Quint and I hadn't spoken, so why was I crying now about how badly our conversation went?

Quint hadn't said anything at all about wanting me to come back. When I told him I felt like I should stay on longer, he had nothing to say at all other than I should do what I thought best. Both of those points only reinforced my earlier resolve.

My tears subsided, and I wiped them from my face. "I really am quite tired, Wellie. I'm going home, but I'll be back to see you tomorrow."

"I'd like that, Darrow."

I stood, kissed his cheek, and thanked him before slipping out the front door.

How had I gotten it so wrong with Quint? I'd been certain that he cared about me. Wren had warned me, though. Not more than three hours ago, she'd said that Quint wasn't the relationship type.

So now what? It was one thing to decide to resolve my life, another thing entirely to know how.

I really had no one to talk to, either. Perhaps Orina, but hadn't she been trying to tell me that I needed to figure my life out on my own?

Wait. There was someone else I could talk to. It had been far too long since I'd spoken with the person who had been my best mate since we were in primary school.

Once I arrived at Covington House, I started a fire, changed into more comfortable clothes, and rang Esland Cartwright, or as I called her, True.

Now that she was a reporter for the London *Times*, we rarely had time to see each other. Well, that and I'd been in America.

"Darrow? My goodness, I was just thinking about you. How are you?"

"Oh, True. You don't know the half of it. Literally."

Even after an hour of getting one another caught up on what had been happening in each of our lives, I felt like I still had so much left unsaid.

"What I'm about to tell you has to stay off the record."

"Of course. What's wrong?"

"There isn't anything wrong. Well, that's not true. There's a lot wrong, but not with this. Sutton, of all people, has fallen hopelessly in love."

"That's wonderful, although I doubt that would've made front-page *Times* news."

I laughed. "Right, except who he's in love with may have."

"Who is it? It isn't a bloke, is it? There'd be hearts breaking all over England if that was the case."

"No, no. He met this woman at MI5. Her name is Finley Harlow, although that's not actually her name. Her real name is Kennedy King-Alexander, but everyone calls her Wren. She was working undercover on the Matthew Caird case."

"Oh, my goodness. To be honest with you, something came across my desk two days ago about this same subject. It wasn't assigned to me, and I was glad of it. The bloke who got it came sniffing around, asking questions about your family. I didn't know why. I guess now I do. You know I wouldn't have told him a thing."

"I do know that, True. That's who I was visiting in the States. She was hiding out. I'm not sure from who or what exactly, other than from Sutton. Anyway, it turns out she was really an agent for the US National Security Agency."

"Bloody hell. This is good stuff, Darrow. Too bad you swore me to secrecy."

"I didn't actually, but I do know that you'd never report on something that I asked you not to."

"I wouldn't. So tell me, what else did you do while you were in America? You were gone for what, three months?"

"About, yes. Well, I fell tits up for Wren's brother, of all people. Turns out he wasn't as keen on me as I was on him."

"Wait a minute. What about Axel?"

"We broke up before I left."

"I don't know what to say."

"Nothing to say, really. I'll always love him. He's as good a person as they come, True. In fact, if you ever find yourself in trouble, he'd be the one to call. No matter what, Axel Fulton is trustworthy."

"I've always thought that about him. I mean, it's been forever since I've seen him. I think the last time was when we went to the football match and I introduced him and Sutton to my father."

"That was a long time ago."

"Yes," True murmured.

"How long has it been?" Both of True's parents had been killed in an automobile accident after visiting their only daughter at university. It was so tragic. Her father had been one of the most popular footballers of all time.

"Eleven years."

"Gosh, True. That long already?"

We talked another half hour and agreed not to let it go so long between again. We also talked about getting together. True told me she'd call and we'd make a plan. I didn't want to push, but part of me wanted to ask if tomorrow would be too soon.

We rang off before I could reveal how utterly pathetic I was. True had fulfilled her childhood dream of becoming a reporter—for the *Times* even. And me? What had I done? Absolutely nothing.

23

Quint

"You need to get the hell outta here for a while," said Deck when I walked into the barn. "Why don't you go back to England with Z for the holidays? Wren isn't comin' back, right?"

I leaned up against one of the travel boxes, folded my arms, and shook my head. I had no idea how to respond. Part of me wanted to tell Deck to mind his own fucking business. "Maybe you should be the one to get outta here for a while," I said instead. "Doesn't Z need you to go with him and do some kind of training, give a briefing on the latest advances in security technology?"

"Nah. I'm good. You, on the other hand, are a pain in everyone's ass."

"Is that so?"

"Yep. Look, everyone understands how hard all of this has been on you, but King-Alexander isn't alone in this. Ranches across Texas suffered the same kind of losses we did. Some not as many, some much worse. It was a natural disaster, Fish. Not a goddamn thing you could've done about it."

I chewed on a piece of straw for a good long time before saying anything. I thought about going back to the house and pretending like this conversation never took place. But Deck was a damn good friend. My best friend. It probably took a hell of a lot for him to say the things he had. And for him to do it, had to mean that things were pretty damn bad.

"Maybe I do need some time away."

"Z told me he was fixin' to leave in the next couple of days."

"That's what he's been sayin'."

"You're gonna go with him then, right?"

I shook my head. "No. Don't think I will, but I'll figure something else out."

Decker stood, looking like he was about to punch something. Instead, he rubbed the back of his neck.

"Darrow's still in England, right?"

"Don't go there, Deck. I'm warnin' you."

He spun around on me. "*For fuck's sake, Quint. Open your goddamn eyes.* And if they are open, pull your head outta your ass." He held up his hand. "Before you even think about saying anything, know this. You have been an ornery *sonuvabitch* since she left. Yeah, losin' all them cattle was hard. It's gonna take us time to recover. But you, my friend, are makin' the biggest mistake of your life if you let her go."

"You done?"

"I reckon I am."

I walked out. I didn't bother telling Decker he was full of shit, because he wasn't. I knew Darrow Whittaker was the finest, sweetest, most loving, smart, funny, and sexy-as-shit woman I'd ever known. None of that changed the fact that I had absolutely nothing to offer her.

If I said the word, she'd come back. I knew it. But for what? To work a damn cattle ranch? She was capable of so much more. In fact, she wanted so much more, and whether or not her brothers or anyone else in her life believed she could do it, there'd come a day when Darrow figured out all on her own that she didn't need anyone else's approval. When that time came, she'd chase her dreams. I wouldn't stand in her way.

It had been three weeks since our last conversation, if it could be called that. I hadn't known what to say to her, and even if I had, talking on the phone just wasn't something I was any good at.

I heard the hurt in her voice when she ended the call, and from that day on, I'd spent every moment trying to tell myself it was for the best that whatever we'd had going when she was in Texas, ended when she left.

"I miss you so much." Those were some of the last words she said to me. Every time I replayed our conversation in my head, that's where I got stuck. I missed her too, probably more than she missed me.

Just like the night I invited her to go to the rodeo in Bluebell Creek, I picked up my phone and called her before I could talk myself out of it. I didn't even bother to figure out what time it was in England, because if I had, it would've given me time to change my mind.

"Quint? Is everything okay?" I could hear the sleepiness in her voice. God, I missed waking up next to this woman.

"Hello, Darrow."

"What's wrong?"

"I've been feeling bad about our last conversation."

"Go on."

"I could make all kinds of excuses, but the truth is, I've never been one to talk much on the phone."

"It took you three weeks to ring me to say that?"

I smiled. "No. It took three weeks of me being a pain in everyone's ass before Deck let me have it."

"Why were you being a pain in everyone's ass, Quint?"

"Because I miss you," I mumbled.

"Sorry, what did you say? I couldn't hear you."

"You heard me. I miss you, Darrow."

"I miss you too, Quint. So what do you think we should do about it?"

"Well, ol' Decker suggested I get away from the ranch for a bit."

"Where do you think you'll go?"

"Z's been talking about heading back to England for Christmas."

"I would really love it if you came with him."

I let out the breath I'd been holding without realizing I was. "Yeah?"

"Yes. You'd better hurry, though. You do know when Christmas is?"

"I don't know exactly when I'll get there, but I promise you this: I'll spend Christmas with you, darlin'."

"I'd like it if you spent more than Christmas with me, Quint. I'd really like you to come stay with me."

"Yeah?"

"Yes. I have a lovely little English manor house on the grounds of Whittaker Abbey where I live all by my lonely self. I'll tell you another secret about it if you'd like."

"I would like that very much."

"The kitchen has been recently outfitted with a coffee maker," she whispered.

"Would you like me to bring some rancher's coffee along with me?"

"You don't need to do that. I ordered a case of it a couple of weeks ago. It arrived yesterday."

I took a deep breath. "Darrow, I know that I don't have much of anything to offer you, and more, I know I don't deserve you bein' this nice to me after how I handled our last conversation, but I just have to say that I can't help myself. I can't stop thinkin' about you."

"I can't stop thinking about you either, Quint."

I wasn't able to get a ticket to go when Z left. Who knew that every flight from Dallas to London would be booked in the days leading up to Christmas? The first availability the airlines had was midday on Christmas Eve. I'd be cutting it close, but as long as the flight was on time and I got through customs quickly and could get a lift to Whittaker Abbey, I'd make it there on Christmas morning.

I'd promised Darrow I'd spend Christmas with her, and I would. I couldn't wait to see the look on her face when I surprised her, but not as much as I couldn't wait to hold her in my arms.

24

Darrow

I poured myself a cup of coffee and sat at the kitchen table, staring at my mobile. I hadn't heard a word from Quint about his travel plans. Z was already back in London. I'd been able to get that much out of Thornton.

If I saw Wren, I'd ask if she'd heard from her brother, but Sutton kept her practically under lock and key.

Quint promised he'd spend Christmas with me, and it was Christmas Eve. I'd gone back and forth about ringing him, finally deciding against it. He'd called to say he was sorry and that he'd come to England. That I hadn't heard from him reinforced my resolve from before his call. As disappointed as I was, this was for the best.

Instead of sitting and staring at my bloody mobile another minute, I turned it off and went to see Wellie.

The next morning, I woke and told myself that it didn't matter that Quint hadn't kept his promise, I'd put a smile on my face and enjoy my day the best I could. It was Christmas, and if nothing else, it would be a lovely day for my nephew and niece. Lilliya was too young to really enjoy it, but Kazmir had confessed that he wasn't sure he'd be able to sleep when I'd kissed him good night.

Instead of going back to Covington House, I stayed the night at the abbey. The only thing I hadn't considered when I went to bed, was that there'd be no coffee served here this morning. I could hurry back to my house and make some, but that would certainly defeat the purpose of staying over. Plus, it would be another reminder that I hadn't heard a word from Quint, and that was something I had to put out of my mind. Or at least try to.

When I made my way downstairs an hour later, I found Wren and Sutton having tea.

"What's this?" I asked after saying good morning and walking over to pour myself a cup.

"Mrs. Mollybock made coffee for Wren," my brother said, raising a brow.

"My goodness. She must like you as much as she likes Sutton."

"How are you, Darrow?" Wren asked, standing to hug me.

"Same as always, it seems. Nothing much ever changes with me. Thank goodness, Orina put her foot down with Mother over Christmas trees this year," I said in my best attempt to change the subject.

"How did she manage it?" Sutton asked.

"She said it would be too confusing for Kazmir."

"And that worked?" asked Wren.

"He's her first grandchild. She'd do anything for him and Lilliya."

"Where's Pinch this morning?" Sutton asked.

"I've no idea."

"That's off again, then?"

I nodded, taking another sip of coffee. "Been off for quite a while, brother."

"I can't keep up."

I caught a look that passed between him and Wren.

"What are you waiting for, darling? Did you have a question for Darrow?"

"I'm not sure it's the right time."

"For what?"

Wren held out her hand to show me the ring on her finger. "I was wondering if you'd be my maid of honor."

"Oh, my goodness! Congratulations!" I shouted. "Of course I will. Oh, I'm so happy for you."

"A Christmas Eve engagement! How romantic," said my mother, joining us along with the rest of the family, who must've come running when they heard my shrieks of joy.

With all the commotion, it was easy for me to slip away from the din and walk over to the window. I was truly happy for Wren and Sutton, and I wouldn't allow my own unhappiness to spoil their day any more than I'd ruin the holiday for everyone else. I turned away from the window and put a smile on my face.

"Darrow?" Thornton called out to me from the entryway.

"Yes?"

"You have a caller."

A caller? Surely Thornton wouldn't refer to Axel as such. What was this about? When I rounded the corner, I couldn't trust my eyes. "Quint? I can't believe you're here!"

I threw my arms around him.

"Merry Christmas, sugar."

"I wasn't sure you'd make it."

"I wanted to surprise you," he said, running his finger down my cheek.

Thornton cleared his throat and excused himself to hang up Quint's coat, leaving the two of us alone in the vestibule.

"I'm so happy you're here," I said, wishing my eyes hadn't filled with tears.

Quint wiped away the single drop that ran down my cheek, then kissed me.

Would that we could walk out the door and be alone, but that would be terribly rude. Not to mention, his sister had just gotten engaged.

"Come and meet everyone," I said, taking his hand.

"I hear congratulations are in order," he said after hugging Wren and shaking Sutton's hand. "I'm Quint Alexander."

"Wilder Whittaker."

"What are you doing here, and how did you know about our engagement?" Wren asked, looking from me over to Z.

Quint smiled. "Yes, Z filled me in, but to be honest, I was worried about you."

"Why?"

"We haven't spoken since right after Thanksgiving."

"It isn't like we do that kind of thing, Quint."

"Would you like a coffee?" I asked when Wren's tone made me uncomfortable.

"I'd love it, darlin'. Thank you."

"Who is this?" asked Orina.

"Wren's brother, Quint."

"You're happy to see him," she said with a wink.

"You have no idea, but, Orina, I haven't forgotten what we talked about."

"When's the wedding?" I heard Quint ask when I brought over his coffee.

"We're keeping it small. Limited to everyone in the room," Wren answered.

"Okay, when?"

"Um…New Year's Eve. Will you be able to stay for it?" she asked.

"Couldn't get me to leave," Quint answered, smiling at me.

"Wellie! What a wonderful surprise," I heard Thornton say in a voice that was louder than necessary. "And, Axel, we had no idea you'd be joining us. Come in, come in."

"Oh, my," Wren whispered, leaning against me and giggling.

I pushed back. "Don't start. If you start, I'll start."

"These two," said Quint. "They get the giggles at the most inappropriate times."

"Come and meet Wellie," I said when I saw Thornton helping him over to a chair.

"Happy Christmas, Wellie." I leaned over to kiss his cheek. "I'd like you to meet Quint Alexander. He's Wren's brother."

"It's a pleasure to meet you, Mr. Alexander." Wellie looked at me and winked. "More than just Wren's brother, no?"

"Yes, Wellie. He is," I whispered, looking up to find Axel staring at me.

"Axel, this is Quint. Quint, Axel."

The two men shook hands, leaving me feeling guilty about how this came about. I had, at least, told Axel there was someone else, but I'd also alluded that it was over. In hindsight, I should've told him Quint was coming for the holiday, but up until a few minutes ago, I hadn't been certain he was.

"You look happy," he said a few minutes later when Quint was talking to his father and Wilder.

"I am, Axel. Although, Quint is merely visiting. I don't intend to return to America when he does."

"No?"

Saying it out loud would continue to reinforce my resolve about needing to figure out my life on my own. "No. And I'm sorry I didn't forewarn you; I wasn't certain he was coming."

"I'll survive. I suppose there will come a day when you're faced with meeting someone I'm involved with."

"Yes, there will," I said, trying to ignore the pain that settled in my chest with his words. I had no right, though. I'd moved on, and Axel would too. "I want us both to be happy, Axel."

He lifted his glass of wine to mine. "Agreed."

"So that's Axel," Quint said later when we'd finished dinner and were getting ready to say good night and go to Covington House.

"Yes. That's Axel."

"He seems like a nice enough guy."

"Are you trying to convince me of that or yourself?"

Quint put his arm around my shoulders and kissed the side of my face. "Jealousy isn't somethin' I have a lot of experience with."

"You've nothing to be jealous about."

He leaned forward so his mouth was next to my ear. "I really want to be alone with you, Darrow."

"Let's say our goodbyes, then."

Quint went to talk to Z, Wren, and Sutton while I thanked Thornton and Orina.

"He seems nice, Darrow," said my brother.

"I think so." I smiled at Orina, who winked.

"Don't be too scarce."

"Ready?" I said after Quint thanked Thornton and Orina.

He leaned into me. "I'm ready, Darrow. Are you?" he whispered.

I knew my cheeks were flaming, but there was nothing I could do about it except smile and make our exit.

25

Quint

"This is hardly a sweet little house, Shadow," I said when we walked inside the front door of the place Darrow had labeled as such.

She smiled at the use of the nickname. "It's smaller than the abbey. It's smaller than the ranch house too."

"Not by much."

I peeked in the rooms that I could see from where we stood. When I turned around, Darrow was standing at the base of the stairs, naked from the waist up.

"Take the rest off," I said, my voice heavy with desire.

As she unbuttoned her slacks, she took one step backwards up the staircase. When she moved the zipper partway down, she took two more steps. When she was halfway up, she shimmied her pants off her hips. Two more steps, she left them where they lay on the stairs.

I climbed to where she was, still facing me. "Panties off, Darrow. Let me see you."

She slid them down her legs, again leaving them where they lay.

"Sit on the top stair," I said, putting one hand on each of her knees and spreading her legs. I knelt in front of her and breathed in her heady scent.

I steadied myself with both hands on her breasts and leaned in closer, blowing cool air on her heat.

"Quint," she breathed, her fingers woven in my hair. "Oh, God," she groaned. "I missed you so much."

I looked up and smiled. "Just this?"

She shook her head, seemingly unable to speak when I tweaked both nipples with my fingers.

"I need you, Quint. More of you."

"What do you need, baby?"

"You. Naked. In my bed." She scooted away from me, stood, and sashayed her sweet body down the hallway with me following right behind. Like her, I undressed as I went.

I stood behind her and pulled her back to my front, nestling my cock against her ass. Darrow gasped. I reached around with one hand and cupped her full breast.

"I'm going to take you hard, baby. I hope you're ready."

Her mewl told me she was. I nipped at the soft skin on the curve of her neck, and she shuddered.

"Get up on the bed, baby, but stay in this position."

I watched, rolling on a condom. An overpowering need to feel her around me without the barrier between us washed over me. Where had that come from? I'd never once had unprotected sex. Why now? Because it was Darrow. The woman I had no business falling in love with, and yet, that's exactly what I was doing. I raised my head and saw her looking at me over her shoulder. I wanted to see her face, her eyes connecting with mine, when I finally, after a month, buried myself inside her.

"Turn over, baby," I said, guiding her with my hand.

Her gaze bored into mine when I rested against her sex. Could she see how much she meant to me just by looking into my eyes?

"Darrow?"

She nodded but didn't speak.

Slowly, I pushed into her, and her eyes closed.

"Look at me," I demanded.

"Quint?"

"There we go," I murmured when I was as deep inside her as I could get, the pressure growing too fast, until I balanced on the precipice. Together, we fell. Waves of pleasure roared through me, and still, our eyes stayed locked together.

I rolled, keeping our bodies joined until we were both on our sides, so close that I could feel her warm breath on my neck.

My mind raged with want to tell her how I felt, but I couldn't say the words out loud. We stared into each other's eyes as if we were at an impasse. Neither knew what to say, so we chose not to say anything at all.

At midnight, I finally let her sleep. I held her soft body snuggled against me while my mind raced and emotions swirled through me. I'd never been in love, yet I felt like I was barreling straight into it with a woman I had no chance of making a life with, and it scared the shit out of me.

It was unseasonably warm two days later when Darrow took me on a tour of the abbey's gardens.

"Would you like to ride?" she asked.

"If you would."

She stopped walking, and since we were holding hands, I stopped too.

"What?" I asked.

"What would you like to do, Quint?"

"Sure, a ride sounds great."

"Never mind."

"Whoa. Wait a minute. What just happened?"

"I have never known you to be indecisive—or disinterested."

"I'm just happy to do whatever you want to do."

"Bullshit," she said, dropping my hand and folding her arms. "If you don't want to be here, say so."

That wasn't it at all, but I wasn't any better at lying than I was talking on the phone, which meant the time had come for me to be honest.

"Come here." I pulled her arms apart and brought her body so it was flush with mine. "We need to talk."

"Bugger me," she mumbled, trying to wiggle out of my hold, but I refused to let her go.

"It isn't as bad as all that," I said, cupping the back of her neck with my hand and bringing my lips to hers.

"Whatever it is, just say it."

"Can we go back to the house?"

"Oh my God."

"Darrow, stop this. You don't even know what I want to talk to you about."

"No one says they want to talk unless it's something bad. Otherwise, whatever it is, they just say it."

I shook my head and released my hold on her. "Look, my sister is getting married in just a couple of days. I don't want to argue with you."

"Is that what we're doing? Are we arguing?" She turned on her heel and stalked off, leaving me standing on the garden path wondering what the hell just happened.

26

Darrow

There would be absolutely no way I would cry. Nope. Wasn't happening. I knew the opening to a breakup; I'd heard it often enough from Axel, and I didn't need to stand around and hear it from Quint.

"Bugger it," I muttered, picking up my pace. Perhaps I could ring Wren and see if Quint could just stay at Dorchester House until New Year's Eve and the wedding. He sure as hell wasn't staying with me if he couldn't wait until after that to end things with me.

What a bloody idiot I was! Orina's words echoed in my head. *Get to know yourself, learn to be okay with yourself. You don't need to be in a relationship to be complete.* That much was obvious since I couldn't seem to stay in one for more than…how long had Quint been here? Three days? *Jesus,* was I that bad?

"Darrow, stop," I heard him say from behind me, but I wouldn't. I couldn't take the humiliation.

"I think you should stay with Wren and Sutton until the wedding," I shouted over my shoulder. "In fact,

Dorchester House is right over there." I pointed toward the forest. "I'll have your things brought over to you."

I felt his hands land on my shoulders. Of course the bastard caught up with me, at six three, he was nearly a foot taller than I was. I tried to shrug away from him, but he held tight.

"Stop, dammit."

"I'll make this easy on you," I said, spinning around to face him. "I'm sorry, Darrow, but this just isn't working out between us. It's been fun, but now it's over."

"Are you finished?"

"Need I go on?"

Instead of answering, Quint kissed me. He thrust his tongue in my mouth as his powerful arms pulled me into him. He lifted me until my legs went around his waist. One hand held my arse while the fingers of the other weaved through my hair, holding me as he deepened the kiss.

"Don't do this," I murmured when he rested his forehead against mine.

"What is it you think I'm doing?"

I shrugged and tried to drop my legs, but he held me where I was. I could feel his hardness press against me. Was he really getting turned on by fighting with me?

"What am I pretending, Darrow? That I care about you? Sorry, I'm no good at pretending or lying."

"If you care about me, why are you ending things between us?"

He let go of my bottom, and my feet landed on the ground. "When did I say I was ending things between us?"

"You said we needed to talk."

"Yep. Sure as sugar did, sugar. Evidently, you filled in the rest of the blanks on your own."

"Go ahead, then. Talk. Whatever you wanted to say, say it now."

"I'd rather wait."

"What for?"

"I don't want to fight with you, sweetheart. All I want to do is go back to the house. Once we get there, I'll light a fire and throw down a blanket near the hearth, slowly—piece by piece—take your clothes off, and then, in the most romantic way I can muster, show you how I feel about you."

"That sounds quite nice."

"Sounds nice to me too."

"I'm sorry, Quint."

"You wanna know how you can make it up to me?"

I nodded.

"March that sweet little body straight home and wait for me near the fireplace."

"What are you going to do?"

"I'm going to watch you walk."

"But I usually follow you."

"Not this time, Shadow."

He spun me around and gave me a gentle nudge. Instead of walking in front of him, I hung back and took his hand. "I am sorry."

"I know you are, and I'm sorry too. If you haven't figured it out by now, I'm not the best communicator there ever was."

I didn't say anything else on the rest of the walk back. Too many thoughts were swirling in my head. Why did Quint say we needed to talk? There had to be something more to it than just him saying he cared about me.

But why had I overreacted? Mainly because I'd been so hurt when I didn't hear from him after that one terribly awkward phone call. And then, I'd struggled on Christmas morning, thinking he wasn't going to show up.

"Tell me what you're thinking right now," he said, stopping right before the gate to Covington House.

"To be honest…"

"Always. Please," he said before I could finish.

"I feel a bit like I'm on a carnival ride."

"In what way?"

I dropped his hand, opened the gate, and went in the front door. Instead of waiting by the fireplace like he'd asked, I went into the kitchen and fetched a bottle of Wellie's brandy. "Fancy a glass?" I asked.

"Sure, if you think it's necessary."

"Wellie always says 'a glass of brandy won't solve your problems; it'll just make finding a solution much easier.'"

"Do we have a problem?"

I carried the brandy into the sitting room and waited while Quint lit the promised fire.

"Where is this going, Quint?"

He knelt on the hearth, stoking it until it was fully ablaze, and then came and sat on the sofa, beside me. "That's why I said we needed to talk."

I took another sip of brandy and turned my body so I was facing him.

"You confessed something to me when you were in Texas."

"Yes?"

"You have dreams, Darrow. The only thing stopping you is your own belief in yourself. You don't need me or either of your brothers to tell you that you can achieve them. You need to believe it for yourself."

I turned back to face the fire. "It isn't that easy."

"Why not?"

"They don't let just anyone into MI6 training. There are a series of interviews required, and to even get the first one takes a referral."

"So ask for one."

I folded my arms and shook my head. "My brothers will refuse."

"How do you know that?"

"Because I already asked."

Quint looked at me like he didn't believe me, but I had. It was a few years ago, but their combined reactions and subsequent refusals were worded in such a way that I'd never ask again.

"That's surprising."

"It wasn't to me."

"Who does the referral need to come from?"

"There's a list of who can endorse a candidate."

"What about Z?"

I'd thought of that, but it seemed unfair to put him in that position when he likely knew that both Thornton and Sutton were opposed.

"Does the person have to be MI6?"

I shook my head. "There's a wide range of candidates, none of whom I know would agree to recommend me."

"What about Wren?"

"No. She wouldn't qualify." I sighed and took another sip. "Look, I appreciate this, Quint, but it isn't just a recommendation. The person endorsing me must believe I'm capable."

"I see."

"Sorry to be blunt, but this is what you wanted to discuss with me? Why I'm not in MI6 training?"

"You know I have to go back to the ranch after the wedding."

"Of course I do."

"I'm not going to ask you to come with me, Darrow."

I stared into the fire, understanding why he said it, and willing my eyes not to fill with tears. There were all kinds of things I could think of to say in response, but every one of them would be reactionary, and not to what he meant. I got it. Quint Alexander wanted me to follow my dreams, just like Orina wanted me to make sure I was whole before I became half of a couple. If I ever became half of a couple.

"I want—"

"Shh," I said, turning to put my fingertips on his lips. "I get it, Quint."

"I'll do anything I can to help you."

"And what if I fail? Will I be too much of a disappointment to you?"

"You know the answer to that." He stood, but I pulled him back down.

"I'm sorry. You're right."

He turned to me, cupped my cheek, and stared into my eyes. "I care about you, Darrow, too much to let you give up your life for mine."

"What if that's what I wanted?"

He leaned forward and kissed me. "If I believed that, we wouldn't be having this conversation."

27

Quint

I hadn't seen Darrow since shortly after we ate breakfast together and she left for the abbey to help prepare for this evening's nuptials.

I couldn't believe my baby sister was getting married. On the other hand, there was no doubt in my mind that Sutton Whittaker was the love of her life.

Like when Darrow had shown up at the ranch, Wren came alive in her future husband's presence. She laughed more, smiled more, even talked more. Her green eyes sparkled when she looked at him in a way that I had never seen.

If the day came when Darrow looked at me in the same way that Wren looked at Wilder, I would know we had a chance. Until then, I'd continue to hold her at arm's length. Was it easy? Hell, no. I talked myself out of it as many times as I talked myself back in.

I wished, like I did so often, that my mama was still alive. She'd know exactly what I was going through. I could ask Z, but my father had been the one to give up his career, at least in part, for his wife. My mother was the one who Z had given everything up for. Did it make her feel guilty? Did she worry that he'd resent her for it somewhere down the line? That's what I wanted to know.

I checked my watch. Soon it would be time for me to join the rest of the guests at the abbey. I went into the kitchen and poured myself a shot of Wellie's brandy, the stuff that everyone seemed to reach for when they were anxious about something. I had to admit, it almost always did the trick. I made sure my tie was straight, and walked out of Darrow's house.

Once again I was overcome by the feeling that everything was about to change. Was it just my sister's marriage, or did the impending shake-up in the universe hit closer to home? As in, between Darrow and me?

Just as I closed the gate behind me, intending to walk to the abbey, a car pulled up.

"Fancy a ride?" Axel asked through an open window.

"Sure," I answered, walking around to get in the passenger side. "Thanks."

"Not at all. I've been meaning to talk to you, anyway."

I scratched my chin and looked out the window. "What about?"

Axel laughed. "How many subjects can you think of that we'd have to talk about?"

"I'd like to come up with about ten or twenty to avoid talking about the one you are."

Axel laughed again. "Look, all I wanted to say is, I think you're good for Darrow."

"Appreciate you sharin' your opinion with me, although I'm not looking for your approval."

He shook his head. "I get that, and I'm not giving it. All I mean to say is, no hard feelings."

"You were ready to let her go."

"What makes you say that?"

"If you weren't, you'd have plenty of hard feelings."

"You're right. Didn't make it any easier, but when it's done, it's done, I suppose."

"You should know I care about Darrow."

Axel nodded.

"You should also know that I'm not going to ask her to come back to Texas with me."

"You likely don't need to ask."

"What I mean to say is, I won't let her come back to Texas with me."

"Why not?"

If Axel loved her, really loved her, he wouldn't need to ask that question.

"Instead of answering, I'll ask one of my own."

"Go on."

"What does Darrow want to do with the rest of her life?"

"I don't know."

"You should ask her."

"Aren't you the one who should be asking her those kinds of questions?"

I shook my head. "I don't need to."

"You're talking in circles now."

"When you figure it out, you'll know what to do."

Axel pulled up in front of the abbey, and a valet approached the car.

"Fancy."

"Standard operating procedure when there's an event at Whittaker Abbey."

"Glad you know what to do."

"There was a time I thought maybe that would be my job."

I studied Axel, who hadn't yet opened his door to get out. "What happened instead?"

He turned to face me and looked me straight in the eye. "I followed my dreams."

"You're catching on."

"What I don't understand is why I should be the one asking Darrow about her dreams."

"Maybe you're the one who can help her achieve them."

I got out of the car and walked toward the abbey's entryway. I looked up and saw Darrow looking at me through a second-story window. When I winked, she smiled.

I'd been thinking about it all afternoon, and Axel giving me a lift only made me more sure of what I had to do. I only hoped it worked.

28

Darrow

The wedding was simple but beautiful. Wren and Sutton made the perfect couple. There was no need for fancy gowns or elaborate preparation; they wouldn't have even needed witnesses. Each other, along with the vicar, would've sufficed.

I was glad that they'd included their families, just because seeing the way they looked at each other gave me hope for my own future.

If there were two people who had the odds against them, they were it, and yet they'd worked it out.

Wren told me earlier, when we were getting dressed, that she'd officially decided to leave her job with the NSA, like Sutton had left his with MI6. Once they returned from their honeymoon in the Maldives, they intended to start their own consulting firm.

First, Thornton had left MI6 when he married Orina. Now Sutton was leaving too. Ironic that I was the only sibling who wanted to spend my life as an agent, and I couldn't even get my foot in the door.

My eyes met Quint's several times during the ceremony, but once it was over, every time I looked for him, he was deep in conversation with Axel.

"Bugger me," I muttered, incredulous that the one man I'd been convinced wouldn't ignore me, was.

"What's wrong?" asked Orina, close on the heels of Kazmir, who was asking his auntie to pick him up.

"You're getting so heavy, Kaz," I said, walking over to a chair to hold him on my lap rather than in my arms.

"Darrow?"

"I heard you." I motioned with my head. "Look at the two of them. Thick as thieves, they are."

"Interesting."

Exactly what I thought, although more than interesting, I found it infuriating.

"Mind if I steal my date?" I asked, putting my arm through Quint's and leading him away from Axel, whom Quint had somehow continued finding his way back to despite my best efforts otherwise.

"Hello, Shadow," Quint drawled.

Flipping heck, he was wankered. Had Axel intentionally gotten him pissed?

"Let's have a seat, shall we?" I said, leading him over to the settee near the fireplace.

"Damn, it's hot in here," he said, loosening his tie. "You wanna get out of some of those clothes, Darrow?" He slipped his hand inside the bodice of my dress.

I rolled my eyes and smacked his hand, which only made him laugh. When he rested his head against the back of the settee and appeared to fall asleep, I tucked a throw pillow under his head and went in search of Axel. I found him in the butler's pantry.

"Hello, Darrow. Fancy a pinch?"

"You're as wankered as Quint is. What's wrong with you?"

Rather than answer, Axel grabbed me and pulled me against him. "Give us a kiss, Dar, for old times' sake."

I tried to wiggle out of his grasp, but he held on tight. "You can't be serious, Axel. Let me go this instant."

Ignoring me, he brought his lips to mine instead. I turned my head only to find Quint standing in the doorway.

"Am I interrupting?" he asked, seemingly far less drunk than he was only a few minutes ago.

"No!" I shouted, trying to get Axel to let me go. When I raised my leg, he did, surprisingly aware, given his state, that I was about to knee him in the knickers.

"You don't have to be like that, Dar."

I pushed past Quint and out of the butler's pantry, expecting him to follow. When I turned around, he and Axel were laughing it up about something, or were they having a row? It was too hard to tell, given their inebriated state.

"Quint? Are you ready to go?" I held out my hand, but he waved me away.

"I got some unfinished business here, darlin'."

He was back to drawling his words. It was different enough that I wouldn't call it slurring.

"Yeah, we have some unfinished business, Dar. Just like you and me."

"Oh, for God's sake," I spat. "Let's go, Quint."

"Hang on, hang on. Ol' Pinch and me are gonna have another drink and straighten out just who you belong to."

"*Belong to?* Did you say 'belong to'? You've got to bloody well be kidding me. You know what? You can both sod off."

"What do you say, Axel? Game of cards, or should we duel at dawn?"

I couldn't believe my ears. This was a side of Quint I hadn't seen before and never wanted to again. In fact, I hadn't seen this side of Axel either, and we'd grown up together.

"I'm leaving, Quint."

"I'll be right behind you, Shadow. No, wait. You're supposed to be behind me."

Both Quint and Axel found that uproariously funny while I was merely disgusted. "Fine. I never want to see either of you again if this is how you're going to behave."

I waited for a response, and when I saw Axel hand Quint a bottle that they both took a swig from, I stormed out of the pantry and out of the abbey.

The sign had come crashing down on my head. Orina tried to tell me, and even Quint had, back before he'd gotten falling-down sloshed. I was on my own. No men. No relationships. No help from my family. Nothing. If I was going to make a life for myself, I'd have to do it all on my own. There'd be no more putting it off. It was the beginning of a new year. There couldn't be a better time to begin a new life.

I asked the valet to give me a lift back to Covington House. "There's a brunch for the wedding couple, in town in the morning. I need to head in tonight to get things set up before they arrive tomorrow."

"I can drive you, Miss Darrow."

"Thank you. I'd appreciate it ever so much. Just give me a moment to grab my overnight valise."

"Would you like me to fetch it for you?" he asked.

"No, it isn't that big, but thank you."

I took the stairs two at a time, grabbed a few clothes, threw them into the bag, and ran back down. I didn't even bother to change.

"Where to?" the driver asked.

"St. Ermin's." If he knew the brunch wasn't being held there, he didn't say a word.

An hour later, he delivered me to the hotel's entryway. When he came around to open my door, I pressed an envelope in his hand. "You didn't see me tonight. Understood?"

He peered into the envelope with wide eyes. "Yes, ma'am. In fact, I've never seen you before in my life."

It took me five days of feeling bloody sorry for myself before I called the one person left who I believed might be able to help me.

"Axel," I said when he answered my call.

"Where in bloody hell are you?"

"Keep your voice down. Is anyone with you?"

"Not at the moment, but everyone is right worried about you."

"I'm fine. I'm at St. Ermin's, and we need to talk."

"I'm guessing you don't want anyone else to know where you are."

"If you do tell anyone, I can promise you, next time I'll disappear for good."

Instead of arguing or telling me I was being melo-dramatic, he simply told me he was already in town and he'd be right there.

Part 2

29

Darrow

While most knew that the British Army, Navy, as well as the Ministry of Defense were located at Fort Monckton in Portsmouth, few knew it was the primary field training center for MI6.

Today, I was at the firing range for rifle practice. Weaponry was an area where I needed more training than others. Most of the trainees in my unit had vast experience; I had none.

With my last shot, I thought I was lined up, crosshairs dead over the center of the target. I reached for the trigger and slowly began to pull, but I couldn't keep the crosshairs steady. Just as the shot broke, I realized too late that I was off target, and it went wide. It was the third time today it happened. What was I doing wrong?

"Tell me the five steps you need to follow," said my instructor.

"Breathe."

"Good. That's one. Elaborate."

"I take a deep breath and let it half out and hold the rest for four to seven seconds while making the shot."

"Is that what you're doing?"

"No, sir. I'm not holding the second half."

"Practice."

"Now?"

"Yes, now. Breathe in deeply and then let out half."

I took a deep breath, then started to exhale.

"Stop!" yelled the instructor.

I held my breath.

"That's it, right there. Breathe normally, Whittaker. You're letting it all out. Don't exhale for more than a second."

"I don't see how this helps the shot."

I could sense the man's exasperation, but he was my instructor; I had to understand in order to learn.

"As you breathe both in and out, your body moves slightly. When you move, you go off target."

He had me practice breathing for another ten minutes. "If you get light-headed, you're holding the second half of your breath too long."

He continued to watch me breathe, no longer counting the seconds along with me.

"Good," he said. "Let's move on. What's next?"

"Relax."

"Correct. Elaborate."

"I need to slacken my muscles."

"Why?"

"Because tension will also cause me to move, but it's bloody hard not to be tense when I'm firing a gun."

"Of course it's hard. But learning how to hit a target is somewhat paramount to why you're here, Duchess." He smiled, which I appreciated.

He put his hands on my shoulders. "Combine the two. Breathe, and then relax your muscles."

Combining the two took far less practice than breathing had on its own. Soon he was asking what was next.

"Aim."

"Right. Make sure you're focusing on the right things, like the front sight. If you are using iron sights, make sure that the front post is centered in the rear sights."

I adjusted my stance and aimed.

"Breathe and relax."

I did.

"Check your crosshairs."

"Still dead-on, sir."

"Good. Get out of position and then get back in."

I did this several times until I wasn't thinking as much as I was doing it innately.

"Next?"

"Slack, sir."

"This is an important step. Watching you, I'd say this is an area you don't need as much practice. Your touch on the trigger is damn near perfect. But tell me why this is important anyway."

"By taking up the slack early, I won't slap, tap, or jerk when the time comes to break the shot."

"Fundamentally, that's correct, and I can tell you, it isn't taking up the slack that throws you off. You go off target earlier than that."

I didn't understand how that was possible. When I took up the slack, I was still aiming.

"Put the four steps together, but don't break the shot."

I went through the exercise in real time, but it felt more like slow motion.

"Where's your aim?"

"Still dead-on, sir."

"When you squeeze, think it through. You're relaxed, holding your breath, have a good sight picture, the slack is taken up, and you're ready to break the shot."

I went through each step in my head, then squeezed the trigger slowly.

"It surprised you."

"The shot?"

"Yes. And that's a good thing. It means you're still in your head, where you need to be. Why?"

"So I stop myself from jumping too much and throwing off the shot."

"Precisely."

I continued practicing, hitting the target dead-on over and over again.

"Your muscles are fatiguing. Let's switch to handguns. Where do we start?"

"Stance, sir," I responded.

"Show me. First, what is your preference?"

"CAR, sir."

"Why?"

"By utilizing the Center Axis Relock, I can move more quickly, and I find the triangle more stable."

"What else?"

"I'm smaller that way."

My instructor laughed. "Yes, but why?"

"Because my shoulders are ninety degrees to the target with my support-side shoulder pointing directly at it."

"Line up your sights."

I brought the gun up so the sights were between my eyes and the target.

"Why else is this position effective?"

"Because I can fire more quickly. My stance doesn't move."

"What's next?"

"Sight alignment and trigger control."

"Both of which you are good at. Now, start breaking shots."

Every shot remained dead-on simply because I was controlling my breathing and relaxing my muscles. An hour ago, neither made sense to me. Now that they did, it was easier to put both into practice.

"You're a damn good shot, Duchess, now that you aren't skipping the first two steps. Keep practicing, but that's all for now. What else is on your schedule for today?"

"Recruiting and handling assets, sir. Following that, surveillance and countersurveillance techniques."

"Good," he said and walked away.

By the time I was permitted to return to quarters that night, I fell asleep without changing out of my clothes.

When I woke the next morning, my arms, shoulders, and head ached. Yet, I'd never been happier at any other time of my life.

I went straight to the firing range after I showered and ate breakfast. I'd only been there an hour when my instructor from the day before approached. I was ready for another lecture about what I was doing wrong. Instead, he told me I'd been summoned to headquarters.

He led me to an all-terrain vehicle and drove me to the building I'd only visited once—when Axel personally delivered me for training.

As we approached, I saw him talking with JohnTwo. *"What in the bloody hell?"* I muttered, wondering what kind of mess I was in now.

"Get her back here as soon as you can," I heard General Pope tell Axel.

"What the bloody hell, Axel?" I said when we were alone.

"I understand that you and Esland Cartwright are close friends. She's in trouble."

"What's happened?"

"A man was found dead in her flat. Whoever killed him left a message for her, saying she was next."

I covered my mouth with my hand. "Oh, God. Poor True."

"I need your help, Darrow."

"Of course. What can I do?"

"Help convince her to trust me."

"I don't understand."

"I'll explain on the way."

"Wait. I'm leaving?"

"As JohnTwo said, I'll have you back as quickly as I can."

Over the course of our two-hour drive north to Bedfordshire, I listened as Axel talked about the woman who had been my best mate since we were children.

Thornton and Orina were waiting under the portico when Axel drove up.

"There she is," said my brother, hugging me. "You gave us all quite a scare."

"I'm sorry for that, but—"

"You needn't say more," said Thornton. "I'll be eternally grateful to Axel for doing for you what Sutton and I should have done."

"Rest assured we'll talk about that another time," I responded, smiling. "Where is True?" I asked Orina after we'd hugged hello.

"With Mrs. Mollybock in the kitchen."

I saw my brother cringe. "Have you ever considered asking her why she doesn't like you?"

Thornton waved me away. Just as well, I couldn't wait to see my friend.

"True!" I shouted, running into the kitchen and finding her talking to the beloved Whittaker family cook. "It's so bloody good to see you. Although I hate the reason why with every fiber of my being."

"I'm so sorry," she said, looking contrite.

"That was always your way, wasn't it? Apologizing for things beyond your control." I released her and hugged Mrs. Mollybock.

"Can I steal her?"

The cook smiled. "On your way, then."

I led her to the east wing and into the bedroom that had been mine as a child and teenager. How many nights had the two of us stayed up talking into the wee hours?

I sat on the bed, pulled True next to me, and fell back on the mattress. "Remember all the hours we spent solving the world's problems? You were going to be the intrepid reporter—well done, by the way, crack reporter at the *Times* before the age of thirty. I always mean to tell you how proud I am of you."

"Thank you," she murmured.

"I was going to be the female equivalent of James Bond. I'm not there yet, but I'm working on it."

"What do you mean?"

"This has to stay so far off the record. You cannot utter it to any other living person."

"I would never, but if you can't tell me…"

"Of course I'll tell you. We're best mates."

"You may not think so much longer," True muttered and fell back on the mattress, beside me.

Whatever she was talking about, we'd get to. But now, I really wanted to talk about myself. Was that horribly selfish?

"Oh, True, please do me the courtesy of begging that I tell you what I've been doing."

"Do tell," she said, albeit with less enthusiasm than I would've preferred.

"I've been at Fort Monckton."

"Fort Monckton?"

"As a reporter, you of all people should know that it's the SIS training site."

"In Portsmouth?"

I rolled my eyes. "No, in *Iceland.*"

"Why?"

"Why am I training there, or why am I in training?"

"Both."

"I suppose it began with me being so bloody frustrated that I was left out of every single conversation that took place between my brothers and Axel. And then it got worse. Losha, Thornton's wife, was a Russian assassin, and as you know, Sutton's wife is a freaking genius NSA agent. Or was. Even my mother is living with Sir Caird—what a scandal that was, right?"

True didn't seem overly interested in the duchess' affair with the former MI6 chief. If I were a reporter, I would be all over that story.

"Anyway, I had enough. Not just with that, but with everything. I escaped to America, came back due to

Wellie's poor health, and in less than a month, my irrelevance was back in full force. And then, on New Year's Eve…"

"What happened?"

"You know Sutton and Wren were married that night?"

"I do."

"Everything was jolly, good fun until Axel and Quint ganged up on me. They were both wankered, and my so-called frivolous approach to life suddenly became their folly."

"Oh, dear."

"Right? Anyway, I was bloody angry and left. Eventually, Axel came looking for me, followed shortly thereafter by Quint. The two got into a pissing match and didn't even notice I'd left again."

"Then what happened?"

"I didn't sleep much at all. I went from feeling as though I finally mastered a certain independence—granted, I was staying with Wren and Quint—but there I was, back in the same spot where I felt as though I'd lost myself. So, I disappeared."

"Where did you go?"

"Nowhere. Wren and Sutton were off on their honeymoon. Quint was off my list anyway, so I ended up getting quite trolleyed at St. Ermin's. Evidently, after several days of unabashed eating and drinking, I called Axel, who came and got me." I sighed. "Always the savior."

"How did you end up at Fort Monckton?"

"Once I sobered up, he listened to me, maybe for the first time. He's the one who got me the training spot. Called in a favor from an old mate who, by the way, is now a bloody general. He gave me a couple of days on my own to think it over, and when I told him it was what I really wanted to do, he made it happen."

"Do you like it?"

"It is training, but yes, I love it."

"I'm sorry he interrupted it."

"You're more important, True." I turned so I was facing her. "There are things you need to know about Axel and me."

"There are things I need to tell you about Axel and me too."

"You have always crushed on him," I said.

"We were children."

My shoulders rose and fell with a deep breath. It was slightly harder to admit that I'd always known Axel had a soft spot for True, or how I'd turned a blind eye to it for so many years. "I know," I whispered. "I also knew he…it…was a bit more for him."

True shook her head.

Perhaps somewhat subconsciously, I put my hand on my heart. "It was, and I always knew it. It shames me to think that I let our friendship drift just to keep the two of you apart."

"He loves you."

"Yes, he does, and I love him, but not in the way you think."

"How, then?"

"So many ways. We grew up together. I can't say he was like my brother, and I doubt he'd say it either. I know now how wrong I was to think we could ever have a romantic relationship, not in the long term anyway," I said, taking a deep breath.

"What makes you say that?"

I fell back against the mattress and looked up at the ceiling. "There are innumerable reasons, but how could I have fallen for Quint so quickly if I was in love with Axel?"

"You know he was at the pub last night."

"What do you mean?"

True lowered her voice. "He was there to wish Wren and Wilder bon voyage. I overheard him tell Axel that he was returning to the States this morning."

I didn't want to accuse True of being daft, but Wren and Sutton were supposed to leave days ago, as was Quint. "Do you know why they were still in town?"

"They were worried about you. Everyone was."

"Flipping heck," I muttered. Why? Hadn't Axel told them I was at Fort Monckton?

"Darrow, are you with Quint now?"

"I'm not with anyone now. I guess you could say that I'm with me. Orina is the one who made me see it was something I had to do," I said, shaking my head.

"How?"

"She told me that she and my brother would never have had a chance if they both hadn't first learned that they could exist on their own. Knew themselves better than they tried to know anyone else. She said she'd come to the realization that she didn't need Thornton, but she wanted him." I rolled to my side. "I didn't know myself at all. I still don't, but I'm working on it."

"I don't know myself either."

True had always possessed a self-assuredness that I envied, even when we first met. Her parents' automobile accident and subsequent death had hit her hard, but she'd come through it with such grace.

"You've known yourself since you were a child. There are those of us who are babes of the universe, like me. I can be totally and utterly clueless. And then there are the old souls. You're one of them. You have wisdom that isn't of your years."

"You give me far too much credit. I am as clueless as any other."

"Axel is an old soul too. I think that's why you connected the way you did, even as children. So tell me, what happened between you?"

"We kissed—almost."

"Nothing more."

"No, nothing more."

"I wasn't asking. I know it was nothing more. You wouldn't allow it to be, because of me."

"Darrow, we aren't...I mean, he's helping me. That's all it is. In fact, doing so is his job."

"Oh, True, you are a silly thing at times. Listen to me carefully."

She nodded.

"I'm not talking about the break-in or even the dead bloke found in your flat. I'm talking about you and Axel."

"If you have a single objection…"

"How could I?"

"I'll gladly stay away from him if that's what you want."

"No, I don't want you to stay away from him, nor do I want him to stay away from you. There is no chance that Axel and I will ever have a romantic relationship again, and that's because *neither* of us wants it."

"That doesn't mean he wants one with me either."

I laughed. "You were right a minute ago when you said you were as clueless as any other, but only in this. Open your eyes, my dear friend, and take a look at the man when he's in front of you. He has the same dazed, love-filled expression you do when you talk about him."

"He doesn't love me, nor I, him. That's ludicrous."

"Maybe not yet, but ultimately, it's what you both want. Especially Axel."

"How do you know this?"

"Because we spent the entire ride from Portsmouth here talking about you."

So much so that he hadn't bothered to tell me that Quint stayed in London because he was worried about me. My assumption was that he'd gone directly home as soon as I left the abbey and went to St. Ermin's.

"What's it like, Darrow? Training, I mean."

I smiled. It was harder than anything I'd ever done, but I'd expected it to be.

"I admire Thornton and Sutton a great deal more now that I'm aware of what they went through. It's bloody grueling."

"Are you allowed to talk about it?"

"Not all of it, but certainly some. Right now, I'm more focused on the physical training, although the mental challenges exhaust me more." I smiled when I remembered telling Quint that one of my professors at Oxford had said that I lacked intellectual incisiveness and analytical skills. According to my trainers who I admitted as much to, the man had been as far off the mark as I was my first few days at firing practice.

"What's your favorite part?" True asked, seemingly more intrigued than she'd been earlier.

"The things I'm best at," I answered, chuckling.

"Like?"

"I never knew this, but it seems that Thornton is known around the intelligence world for his stealth. Part of that is training, but everyone has innate abilities that manifest in a person wanting to become an agent. I'm quite good at that, apparently. And while I was bloody awful at shooting a gun and had never done it, in the last two days, I find I'm mastering it quite well."

"You really do love it," said True. "It wasn't just folly."

"Quint is the one who saw it first. Even when I told him, and myself, that I didn't have what it took to become an agent, he told me I was wrong. I don't know for certain, but I suspect he put a bug in Axel's ear about endorsing me even before my grand disappearance."

"He must care for you, Darrow."

"That's just it. He told me he cares for me, but he also told me that he wouldn't ask me to come to Texas. He insisted I pursue becoming an officer, even if it meant we couldn't ever be together."

"Surely, after you've completed training—"

I shook my head. "While I hate the unfair generalization of what I'm about to say, it remains true. It's harder for female agents to maintain relationships than it is for their male counterparts, especially in MI6. There were years our family rarely saw Thornton. It wasn't quite as bad with Sutton, but he was MI5. I don't know how much you know about Quint's life or family, but he owns a hundred-thousand-acre ranch in Texas."

"That's where you went last year."

"It isn't something he can walk away from."

"I'm sorry, Darrow."

I took a deep breath and squared my shoulders. "Don't be. It's my decision, and as I told you before, I have to find out who I am, pursue my dreams. I would be filled with regret if I didn't, and that wouldn't contribute to a happy relationship of any kind."

"I understand. It remains tragic, though."

"Enough about me. As far as what you're going through, all I can say is trust Axel, and do whatever he tells you to do."

"Listen to her."

When I heard Axel's voice coming from outside the bedroom, I wondered how much he'd heard. Instead of looking over at him, I studied my friend.

"What?"

"You've done the right thing, True. You just need to see it through."

"I'd forgotten that's what you used to call her," said Axel, walking into the room and over to the window. "Why did you?"

"My name means true," she answered.

I jumped up, suddenly feeling like a third wheel. "I haven't seen Wellie, yet. I think I'll go do that. I mean, unless there's something else you need me for, or if I'm not allowed to."

"What are you going on about?" Axel asked.

"When are we going back to Monckton?"

"Not until tomorrow."

I clapped my hands, leaned down, and kissed True's cheek. I'd hoped he wouldn't keep me here much longer. As it was, I got enough ribbing about special treatment. Little by little, I was earning the respect of my fellow trainees—men and women I'd work with for the rest of my life. I couldn't afford to backpedal and have them believe I wasn't as committed as they were.

As I walked the distance to Wellie's cottage, I wondered if Quint's plane would still be in the air. It was a nine- to ten-hour flight, longer if he had a layover somewhere. Before I talked myself out of it, I pulled my mobile out of my pocket and rang him.

"Shadow, this is an unexpected call. Is everything all right?"

"Hi, Quint. Everything is fine, other than what's happening with True, but I understand you know something about that."

"True?"

"Sorry. Esland Cartwright."

"I don't know much. Listen, I don't have much time. My flight from Chicago is about to board. What can I do for you?"

"I'm at the abbey, but only overnight. Axel needed my help with something, so he got me a day pass." I laughed, and so did Quint. "Anyway, the reason I called was to thank you."

"I didn't do anything."

"Your response tells me you did, Quint, and I appreciate it. If nothing else, you gave me the push I needed. I suspect you did more by way of Axel."

He didn't say anything, but I could hear the din of the busy airport in the background.

"Quint?"

"I won't apologize, Darrow. Not that you're asking me to."

"I miss you and I will continue to, but I know this is for the best."

"It is. You'd never be happy if you didn't pursue becoming an agent."

"Goodbye, Quint."

"Goodbye, Shadow. I wish you the best of luck in everything you do. I mean that sincerely."

I rang off before letting on that I was crying. How could I not? Something inside told me I'd never again see the man who I knew was the great love of my life.

30

Quint

There were so many questions I wanted to ask Darrow, and with six hours left in my layover, I certainly would've had time, but for what reason?

Before I left London, I'd had a long talk with Z about her. I hadn't initiated it; my father had.

"You care about Darrow," Z had begun.

"Where are you goin' with this?"

"The life she's about to lead is far different than I think even she understands. It's different now than it was when I first became an agent."

"I think she understands that, Z. She's watched her brothers live it."

The look on my father's face had been skeptical, but even if it was different, Darrow would adapt. I loved the resolve I heard in her voice when she'd called a few minutes ago. And while I'd heard the same sadness I was experiencing, it seemed we both knew this was for the best. Better now than if she hadn't told me what she wanted to do with her life in the first place, or had stayed on longer in Texas, or if she'd come back with me. The longer we perpetuated a "relationship," the harder it would be on both of us to end it.

This way, the break was clean and we could move on with our lives.

I couldn't say I was looking forward to getting back to the ranch, but I also knew that once I was there, my life would fall back into the same easy rhythm it always did. I might even consider going out more often, maybe dating with some kind of regularity. Although, what woman alive could hold a candle to the formidable Darrow Whittaker? There probably weren't any.

31

Darrow

I wiped my tears before walking to the front door of Wellie's cottage. I didn't want him to think I was upset about Axel and True, because I wasn't.

I'd expected to feel something when he started talking about her on the drive from Fort Monckton to Bedfordshire, but other than being happy for him and for my friend, I didn't feel much of anything.

My conversation with Quint, on the other hand, had left me feeling as though I had a giant hole in my chest. Could it really be that I'd never see the cowboy again?

I'd see him, of course. My brother was married to his sister, but outside of family gatherings made more infrequent given he lived in Texas and everyone else was in the UK, when would I actually have an opportunity to see him? I'd hardly bump into him while undertaking a mission.

"Good afternoon, lass," said Wellie, sitting in the same chair I'd so often found him in.

"Hello, Wellie. It's so good to see you," I said, leaning down to kiss his cheek.

"Sit down and tell me all about Fort Monckton."

I smiled. I should've known Axel would tell his father about where I was and why.

We'd talked for less than an hour when the man himself walked into the cottage.

"Change of plans, Darrow. I'm sorry, but I'll need to take you back this afternoon," he said after greeting his father.

"There isn't much left of the afternoon," Wellie commented.

"Right. As I said, I'm sorry."

"No matter at all, really. I'm anxious to get back."

Axel looked relieved. He really had no idea how much this opportunity meant to me, did he?

"This isn't a chore I'd rather not do," I said to him. "It's the beginning of a new life for me."

When I looked at Wellie, tears formed in my eyes. The way he looked back at me, as though he couldn't contain his pride, meant everything.

"Let's be gone, then," Axel said, coming around to kiss his father's cheek as I'd done. It was something I'd always admired about father and son. I couldn't remember a single time Thornton or Sutton had ever kissed our father's cheek.

Back at the abbey, I said goodbye to Thornton and Orina and climbed in the back seat of Axel's 4x4.

"I can sit in the back," True offered.

I ignored her and closed the door, but from where I sat, I could see the kiss my friend and Axel shared. I doubted he'd ever kissed me that way.

"You two are explosive," I said to True when she got in the front seat and Axel closed her door.

"I'm sorry. That was insensitive."

"Hot is what it was."

"You take good care of True," I said when Axel parked near the main building of Monckton and I hugged him. "And you, do as he says, but only to the extent of it keeping you safe. Otherwise, make him work for your love."

True smiled, the first I'd seen in over an hour. "Thank you," she murmured before hugging me one more time and getting back into the 4x4.

"Welcome back, Duchess," said General Pope, who I hadn't seen walk up.

"Thank you, sir. I really didn't want to leave in the first place."

"Have a seat," he said, pointing to a bench near the walkway. "It's something you'll get used to—having to leave even when you don't want to."

"Yes, sir," I murmured.

"Before you return to your quarters, I want you to know that you're making remarkable progress. Given the circumstances of your arrival, you may have experienced unfair prejudice, not just from your fellow trainees, but from some of our instructors as well. You've navigated both bravely, and for that, I commend you. Continue to work hard, Whittaker. Nothing will be handed to you, but you will earn the same opportunities as everyone else."

"I appreciate your kind words, sir."

"Off you go, then. Long day tomorrow, given you'll need to make up what you missed today."

Three days later, I was once again at the firing range when I heard my name echo over my cadre's radio.

"Whittaker, let's go. You've been summoned to headquarters," he yelled out to me.

The same ATV transported me back, but instead of seeing General Pope talking to Axel, this time it was with Z. When I joined them, we went inside.

"You'll be leaving with Chief Alexander shortly after the conclusion of this meeting," the general began.

"You're aware of the situation with Esland Cartwright?" said Z.

"I am."

"We believe the threat has escalated. Cartwright is being transported out of the country tomorrow morning," said General Pope. "You'll be on her detail."

My eyes opened wide despite doing my best not to react.

"Look at this the way it's intended, Whittaker. Getting your first assignment this early in your training is an honor you've earned," Pope added.

"Do you have any questions?" asked Z.

I did, but I'd ask them once we left Portsmouth. "No, sir," I said to Z before turning to General Pope. "Thank you, sir."

"Go ahead and ask; I know you're dying to," said Z once we were in the car on our way to the abbey.

I smiled and sighed. "Is this a real assignment, Z?"

"It is, and you should take it as such. What I am about to tell you means you've been granted the appropriate level of security clearance. Pinch and Esland have been able to determine the reason her life was threatened. The investigation will be taken over by MI5, and we'll begin to move on it as soon as she is safely out of the UK."

I looked out the window of the vehicle and thought a long time about what I wanted to say. The last thing I wanted anyone to think was that I didn't appreciate the opportunities I'd been given. However, there was no way I was ready to take on an assignment. Perhaps they were thinking of letting me go from the training, and the best I could hope for was bodyguard-type detail, likely for those in my "social class."

"You have a little over an hour to tell me what has your brow so furrowed, young lady. Once we're in the presence of the other agents, you will not have such easy access to me."

Z was smiling, but would he still be if and when I expressed my doubts?

The first thing I did once we arrived at Whittaker Abbey was visit Wellie. Since I hadn't had the nerve to express my doubts to Z, perhaps I could get the counsel of a man I trusted implicitly to be honest with me.

"Back so soon?" he said when I knocked, then entered the cottage.

"My sentiments as well."

I told him about my day thus far. As he listened, Wellie brushed his finger over his lips.

"I wonder, given her importance to Axel as well as the Whittaker family, if they would be so cavalier with her life."

"What do you mean?"

"I'm saying that if all you're good for is to be a bodyguard, and one not taken terribly seriously, if Z finds Esland expendable."

"Of course he doesn't," I snapped.

"One would think, then, that you'd be proud to take on this duty, lass."

"I am, Wellie. Quite proud."

"I'm going to say something to you, and I want you to listen without responding."

"Okay."

Wellie leaned forward and grasped my hands in his. His bones were gnarled by arthritis, and the skin was scarred from his years of landscaping work. "You, Darrow, have always questioned your own worth. Granted, I'll acknowledge that you didn't always see a place or purpose for yourself. But those of us who have known you all your life, believed you would one day do great things. I've believed that since the day you were born. You were less than a week old when the duchess invited me to the abbey to meet you. It was one of the proudest moments of my life when she invited me right into the sitting room and put you in my arms."

"I never knew she'd done that."

"She told me that day that she expected me to look out for you. She also told me that she knew she could count on me to love you like you were my own."

I laughed through my tears. "I have to tell you, Wellie, that doesn't exactly sound like my mother. Did she do the same with Thornton and Sutton?"

Wellie's gaze remained steadfastly serious. "She didn't. You were different, Darrow."

"Thank you for telling me that."

"When you leave tomorrow, I want you to remember every word. I, for one, am terrifically proud of you."

Later that evening, when everyone was at dinner, my oldest brother stood with glass in hand and faced me.

"I'd like to begin by making a toast to my sister. I've never been prouder of you, Darrow. I may be retired; however, I will still welcome you to Her Majesty's Service."

I raised my glass as well in the midst of several "hear, hears."

"I don't recall getting an assignment while in training," Thornton added, looking between Axel and the other MI5 agent who had taken a seat during the toast. "What about the two of you?"

"I barely made it through training," the man admitted, laughing at himself. "Congratulations, Darrow."

"I'm not entirely finished. Once I've completed my current assignment, JohnTwo has called for my return to Fort Monckton."

"There is another possibility," said Thornton, taking a seat and brushing his lower lip with his finger like Wellie had done earlier.

"Do tell, Thornton," I said, leaning forward.

"You could continue training in the US."

"More details, please."

"I'll get back to you on that. However, on that same subject, you'll be meeting Mantis and Alegria at the airfield at zero six hundred. I don't yet know who else they're sending. It's no matter, really. You'll find out in the morning."

An hour later, I noticed True yawn at the same time Axel did.

"Ready to call it a night?" he asked.

"I hate to be a spoilsport."

"Let me, then," Axel said, looking around the table. "We have an early departure tomorrow."

"We do," I added, standing at the same time the man who had been introduced as Edge did.

True and I made eye contact; something was bothering her. Before I could ask what, I overheard her ask Axel if their staying in the east wing of the abbey would be awkward. I had to assume it was because I was there.

"I'm on my way to Covington House to pack, so no, it won't be awkward at all," I told her.

"Don't be an imp," Axel scolded.

"You are not the boss of me," I teased. "Oh, wait. Perhaps you are. I hadn't thought of that."

32

Quint

"There's more," my father said when he called to tell me about Axel bringing Esland to the ranch.

"Get on with it, Pa," I said, laughing at my father's typical approach to telling me something he feared I might balk about.

"Darrow Whittaker will be on her detail."

"Darrow? Didn't she just start her training?" I didn't know what to make of my father's news. "She hasn't dropped out, has she?"

"Nothing of the kind. In fact, this is her first official mission."

"Not that I doubt her ability but, Z, isn't this a little soon?"

I heard my father sigh. "If you didn't doubt her ability, you wouldn't have asked the question, Quint."

Z was right.

"When she arrives, I'd take it as a personal favor if you'd refrain from expressing your opinion."

"Don't get mad. I was just surprised."

"Right. I'll see you tomorrow evening."

Z ended the call, leaving me feeling like an asshole, and rightly so. Why had I been surprised? When Darrow was here at the ranch, she'd picked up on everything Wren and I taught her faster than anyone else I'd ever known. Much of it she hadn't needed to be taught; she'd figured it out intuitively.

There were few outside of the permanently employed ranch hands who had any idea how elaborate the security systems were at King-Alexander. They'd been installed years before when my mother was still alive and Z lived here.

Deck had taken over the ranch's security when Z returned to London, and updated the systems regularly. When Wren came back last year, though, Deck had insisted it go through a major overhaul.

In-ground sensors had been installed throughout the property and were used to detect physical movement, acoustic signals, and vibrations. In addition, a multi-drone surveillance system that made use of thermal sensors capable of approaching areas of interest once a further investigation command was given.

Each of the ranch's buildings, including the main residence, were secured with the latest in surveillance and facial recognition capabilities.

Visitors to the ranch who would not need to have access beyond a certain number of hours or certain buildings, were automatically scanned upon arrival. I'd yet to have someone flagged as a security risk, but I secretly found myself hoping one day I would, just so I'd get to see what happened.

Deck and I had met some of the K19 team members then, when they'd come to install the new systems, and while Burns Butler hadn't come along, Decker told me he'd designed the whole of it.

He would be contacting Burns today about adding three assets—Axel, Esland, and Edge—and I hoped he'd let me help or at least watch. I loved the little glimpses I got into the world my best friend, father, and sister operated in, and while I wouldn't want it to be my career, playing in the spy game from time to time was fun.

After being on video chat with the man for more than an hour, Decker was about to end the conversation, when Burns mentioned that Darrow would be continuing her training with him and a man named Leech Hess once the Cartwright mission was complete.

I shook my head and smiled. I was so damn proud of her, not that I had any right to be. She'd done this all on her own. I couldn't wait to congratulate her in person.

A few hours later, I got my wish when I received an alert from the front gate. I went outside and waited as they drove up. Axel exited the SUV first and held his hand out to Esland, who followed. Darrow and Edge exited from the other side.

"Welcome," I said when Axel and the woman I recognized as Esland walked over to me. I shook both of their hands.

"This is Edge," said Axel. I recognized him as well from the profile I'd uploaded. After we shook hands, I looked behind him to the person I wanted to see more than any of the others—more than anyone else on earth, actually.

"Welcome back," I said to Darrow as we walked toward each other. Once I was close enough, I took her in my arms and spun her around in a circle.

I stopped moving but didn't let her go. Having her body flush against mine felt too damn good. When I put one hand on her ass, Darrow wrapped her legs around my waist.

"I want to kiss you," I said.

"What's stopping you?"

I had my back to the house. "Do we have an audience?"

"We don't, not that it would stop me from kissing you."

I captured her mouth with mine and weaved my fingers into her long hair. "God, I missed you," I whispered, regretting saying the words out loud as soon as I had.

She leaned back, put her hands on either side of my face, and looked into my eyes. "I missed you too."

I slid her down my body. "Z tells me you're doing great at Monckton."

She shrugged and turned away, but not before I caught the hurt look on her face. I grabbed her arm and spun her around to face me. When she looked into my eyes and smiled, I forgot everything I'd planned to say. Instead, I kissed her again.

"Feed me dinner and then take me to bed, cowboy," she said, pulling me by the hand.

"Who flew you in?" Deck, who had joined us, asked Axel when we sat down at the table. "Mantis and Alegria?"

"That's right."

"I'd hoped to reconnect with them."

33

Darrow

I was puzzled. How did the ranch manager know the two K19 operatives?

"They had to fly to California to pick up whoever K19 is sending this way," Axel explained and then turned to me. "I was telling Ezzie that you've met Merrigan Shaw."

"Right," I answered, looking at True rather than Axel. "Did you know that Sir Caird originally asked her to take over as chief of MI6?"

"It wouldn't surprise me," True responded. "Her accomplishments are legendary. I told Axel I'm envious you've met her. I hope I get to one day."

"You should reach out," I suggested.

Axel's reaction to my words seemed odd. Maybe he already had.

Quint ran his finger over the back of my hand. "Tell me more about your training."

I leaned forward so my mouth was next to his ear. "I'd rather we just call it a night, Quint." When I tilted my head and kissed his neck, he shuddered. When I looked up, we were the only two left at the table.

I got up and began taking our dishes to the kitchen.

"You don't have to do that," Quint said.

"I don't mind."

He got up and began loading the dishwasher while I put away the leftover food.

"I like this," I said.

"Cleanup duty?"

I walked over and put my arms around his waist. "Being here with you, having it feel…normal between us." I put my fingers on his lips. "Before you say anything, I know this is…temporary."

I offered to ride out with Quint, but he told me to go back to sleep.

"Don't forget why you're here," he reminded me.

He was right. I wasn't here for a visit; I was here because True's life was in danger and I was one of the people tasked with keeping her safe.

"I'll be back as soon as I can," he said, giving me another kiss.

"Wait," I said when he was almost to the bedroom door. "Give me another one of those."

He smiled, walked back to the bed, leaned down, and kissed me again. "The sooner I get out there, the sooner I'll be back."

As hard as I tried to go back to sleep, I couldn't. I got up and went out to the kitchen. When Quint did come back, I'd have a full breakfast waiting.

"Good morning."

I startled when True walked in. "Good morning," I said with my hand on my heart. "How did you sleep?"

"I slept fine, but who are you?"

I laughed. "I slept quite well too, thanks. Coffee or tea?"

"Tea, please."

"Have a seat. It'll just be a minute."

"Darrow Whittaker, I've known you most of my life, and you are not a morning person."

"I know," I said, sitting next to her. "It's just that when I'm here, I am. I mean, God, Quint and the rest of the ranch hands are up before dawn. If I sleep until eight, I feel like a sloth."

"Wow." Esland shook her head. "Are you two, you know, together?"

We were, for now. Without having discussed it, there seemed to be an unspoken agreement between us that we'd live in the present and not think about what might happen in the future. "For now, we are. When I go back to England, I've no idea what will happen. And after, well, I am training to serve SIS in some form."

"What about training here, like your brother mentioned?"

"We'll see." I didn't want to get my hopes up, but even if I did train in the States, it would only be for a short while. I'd still have to return to England to complete MI6 training.

I stood when the teakettle whistled. "Where is Axel? Still sleeping?"

"No, making calls."

There was a time when needing to leave the room while Axel "took care of business" drove me mad, and I said so. "Does it bother you?" I asked.

"I suppose it depends on whether Axel stays true to his word and lets me work on the investigation alongside the rest of you."

"Is that a possibility?"

True nodded. "In fact, he has something for us to work on together."

"Who us?"

"You and me."

"You're joking?"

"I'm not."

I rested my elbows on the table. "Well done, my friend. I admit, I didn't think he had it in him."

"I thought you said she never uttered a disparaging word about me," Axel said to True. I averted my gaze when he kissed the back of her neck. "Where's Quint this morning?"

"He should be back soon," I said, looking at the clock. "He typically comes in for breakfast about this time." I stood, walked back over to the kitchen, and began pulling food from the refrigerator.

"Are you cooking breakfast?" Axel asked.

"Watch it," I said, raising the pan I'd just gotten out of the cupboard. "Quint thinks I'm an excellent cook."

"Good morning," said Edge, joining us at the dining table. "Quint and Decker said they'd be in as soon as he washes up."

"Did you ride out with them?" I asked and he nodded.

A few minutes later, Quint came inside with Deck. "What's this? A full breakfast?"

I smiled and kissed him.

"Did you visit your hens this morning as well?"

"I did." I showed him the three cartons of eggs sitting on the counter.

"I don't know how she does it, but Darrow somehow manages to get three times the eggs from those hens as I'm able to. Even Tee-Tee doesn't round up that many," Quint said, putting his arm around my shoulders.

True and Axel both looked stupefied.

"Tee-Tee is the Alexanders' version of Mrs. Mollybock," I explained, but neither of their expressions changed.

"Oh, come on," I groaned. "Is it really that surprising that I know how to gather eggs? Your own father taught me, Axel."

"I am not aware of any such thing ever happening."

"Sod off, Fulton," I muttered, sitting down next to Quint. "What's the plan for today?"

"The K19 team will arrive shortly after eleven hundred hours," said Axel.

"Who's coming?" Quint asked.

"I'm not entirely certain."

Axel was lying. I wondered why.

Something passed between him and True, which I chose to ignore. "Can I get you another cup of coffee?" I asked Quint.

"I can get it."

"I know, but I can too." I stood and took both of our cups to the kitchen. When I came back, they were still discussing who was coming from K19. I looked at Quint, who rolled his eyes.

"All right," said Axel. "Ranger and Diesel. Do those names mean anything to you?"

True shrugged, picked up her fork, and continued eating. "This really is fabulous, Darrow. Well done."

"True tells me there's an assignment for us to work together," I said, hoping to break the strange tension in the room.

"Right," said Axel, finishing the last bite of food on his plate and looking at Quint. "Call is yours, mate. If you prefer I not talk missions around you, I'm happy not to, but on the other hand, you've been around this business all of your life."

"You never offered me the same courtesy," I grumbled, wondering why Axel would talk so freely in front of not just Quint but Decker, the ranch manager, too.

Quint reached over and rubbed my shoulder. "And if he had, maybe you wouldn't be livin' your dream, darlin'."

I leaned over and kissed his cheek.

"I don't mind either way," Quint answered Axel. "Just so you know, I do have third-level clearance."

Axel raised a brow.

"I facilitated getting him cleared through the agency," said Decker.

"Esland has recently learned of a trust originally put in place by Lord Maxwell Westbrook, her great-grandfather."

I looked between Decker and True. I was unsure which of the last two bits of information surprised me more, that Decker either now worked for the CIA or had in the past, or that True was related to Lord Maxwell. "Max is your grandfather?"

"He is," True answered.

"Why didn't you ever say?"

She shrugged. "It never came up."

"Anyway, this trust is significant," Axel continued. "Shiver received intel suggesting there may be another heir. He has no further information, other than this heir would only inherit upon Esland's passing."

I took a breath and sat back in my chair instead, waiting for Axel to continue.

"Given that, Shiver believes there may be a threat potential. Also, given that Esland's mother was an only child as was her grandmother, the heir would have to be descended from a sibling or even cousin of Lord Westbrook himself."

"Is this our project?" I asked True.

"Yes. I was thinking we could start with genealogy."

Axel asked Decker to show us how to access the network and which to use. He then explained how the biorecognition access points worked before everyone but Quint and I left the room.

"You're smiling," he said, pulling me onto his lap.

"I'm…what's the expression? Geeking out a bit."

"It is pretty cool. You know who set it all up, don't you?" Quint asked, laughing.

I shook my head.

"Deck and Burns Butler."

"Goodness," I muttered. What I'd give to be in a room with him for five minutes. Not to mention I was still stunned by Deck's involvement.

"I hate to say this, but I need to get back out there."

"I know," I sighed, wishing I could ride out with him. "Where did True run off to?" I asked, looking around the room.

"She and Axel went that way." Quint pointed to the bedroom.

"I'll walk you to the barn." I followed him out.

"It's nice having my shadow with me," he said when I walked with him over to Gunsmoke's stall.

"Would that I could follow you around all day. Sadly, I am on duty."

"It's what you wanted, Darrow."

"I know, and I'm not complaining. Not really anyway. It's the same as when you said you hated to say it, but you need to get back out here."

"Exactly," he said, pulling me into his arms. "I heard a rumor you might be interested in."

"What's that?" I smiled at the twinkle in his eye.

"Doc Butler is on his way here. You may already know that."

"I didn't."

"Then, you probably don't know that he'll be talking with you about training with K19."

"And you know this, how?"

"You'd be surprised what all I know." He nuzzled my neck and pulled my body against his. "You know that part about me hating that I have to ride out? I'm hating it even more right now."

"Speaking of how you're so well informed, where is Decker?" I asked, looking around the barn.

"He left a little while ago and will be out of town for a few days."

I wiggled my brows, led Quint into the office, and locked the door behind us.

"What is your intention, ma'am?" he said, taking off his hat and putting it on the desk.

"I have some interrogation techniques I'd like to practice on you."

"I always wanted to be someone's homework. Where do we start?"

"Take off your clothes, cowboy."

"You first," he said, unbuttoning his shirt.

"Excuse me, Mr. Alexander, I am the one doing the interrogating today. I'll be making the rules." I stood in front of him and unfastened his belt.

"I kinda like this."

I dropped my hands. "Quint...I..."

"Come here," he said, pulling me onto his lap. "What's goin' on, Darrow?"

"How can two things that are so far apart both feel so right?"

He cupped my cheek. "I don't know the answer, sweetheart."

"I love being here with you."

"I know you do, and I love having you here, but—"

"Don't say it." I tried to get up, but Quint held tight.

"I am going to say it, and you're going to listen. Everything you've ever dreamed of is within your reach. Think about that for a minute. You're actually *doing* what you've always wanted to do. I can't be the man who takes that away from you. I couldn't live with myself."

"It's ironic that if it weren't for you, I wouldn't be doing this at all." I rested my head on his shoulder.

"Let me ask you this. Would you ask me to leave Texas, leave the ranch, and move to England?"

I sat up straight and looked into his eyes. "Of course I wouldn't. This is your life. It's everything you love."

He didn't need to say another word; I got what he was trying to tell me.

I lost track of time as we sat and held each other. God, I loved this man. Thinking it, ripped my heart to shreds. Saying it out loud would destroy me.

"They're here," Quint said when an alert popped up on his phone.

"Do we have to go and greet them?"

"Nope," he said, holding me tighter.

"You have to get to work, though."

"Not just yet," he said as he unbuttoned my blouse.

Both of our phones buzzed with a message that Doc Butler was looking for me.

"Duty calls," said Quint, winking as he helped me back into my clothes before putting his on. "I'll never look at this office the same way again."

I would've said I wouldn't either, but would I ever actually see it again after the next few days?

"Go ahead," he said, noticing I was waiting for him. "I'll catch up with you later."

When I walked out, Edge was waiting with two men I didn't recognize.

"This is Ranger Messick and Diesel Jacks. Both men are with K19."

"I understand you'll be training with us," said the one Edge introduced as Diesel.

"I've heard a rumor," I said, smiling. "I'm actually on my way to meet with Doc now."

"Do you know where—"

I guessed Edge was about to ask after Quint when the door to the office opened and he walked out.

"Gentlemen," he said, looking between the three men and me. "What can I do for you?"

"Thought we'd ride out with you this afternoon," Edge said.

I saw this as the perfect opportunity to leave. "I'll catch up with you later," I said, waving as I walked out of the barn and over to where I saw Doc on the front porch.

"Hi, I'm Darrow. I've heard a lot about you. I'm sorry if I kept you waiting." I held out my hand and shook his.

"I'm Doc, or Kade as you'll hear Merrigan call me. And you didn't. Axel and I just finished up." Doc motioned for me to have a seat.

"I must confess that I feel mildly uncomfortable at the moment. If you were coerced into—"

"Stop right there," he said, holding up his hand. "No one coerces me into anything. Well, Merrigan does sometimes." He winked. "But not in this case. I had a conversation yesterday with JohnTwo. He expects you'll soon be bored with MI6 training."

My face fell. Is that really what the commander thought of me? I'd approached every task, every lesson, every exercise with enthusiasm and a desire to learn, and yet it hadn't been enough.

"Look at me, Whittaker."

"Yes, sorry. I'm just embarrassed that I've failed so miserably."

"Interesting," he said, scratching his chin.

"What?"

"General Pope told me your instincts were 'spot on,' as he put it. But in this instance, you couldn't be more inaccurate."

"Sorry. I'm not following."

"He thinks you'll be bored because you are exceeding your trainers' expectations. JohnTwo thinks you need more of a challenge."

"Oh," I mumbled, trying to mask the smile spreading across my face.

Doc leveled a serious gaze on me. "You're being given a unique opportunity to train with K19 Security Solutions, in part because of my relationship with your brothers, but not solely. You've earned this, Darrow, and I expect you to continue earning it."

"I appreciate it, sir."

"Do you have any questions?"

"What exactly will I be doing?"

"Each member of the K19 team brings with him or her a certain level of expertise in intelligence and security. Some specialize beyond that, based on their prior careers in the military, with the CIA, and in some instances, both. Once your general training begins, any skill or skills that you innately excel at will be identified. Your training in those skills will be intensified."

"It sounds daunting."

"It is. Not to cast a shadow on MI6 training, but this is...better. I'll warn you; no one will go easy on you."

"I wouldn't want them to."

"Of course you wouldn't, and that's one of the reasons I agreed to do this."

"I don't know what to say, other than to thank you."

"Your thanks to me will be in your hard work. Don't make me give Shiv a bad report."

I shook my head and laughed. "I won't. I promise."

"Your brother is one of my closest friends. Merrigan's too."

"I met her through Thornton."

We continued to talk about his wife and my brother, MI6, and finally about the current mission.

"This is nasty business, Darrow. The people responsible for killing Tommy Sholes will stop at nothing to kill Esland as well. Who knows how many others have been killed in ways that, like Esland's parents, were considered accidental. When there are billions of dollars—or pounds in this case—on the line, people are driven to do horrific things."

"Understood." I didn't know Mr. Sholes, other than that he'd played on the same team as True's father. I'd seen photos of the crime scene, and what the killers had done to the man was heartbreaking and gruesome.

"Merrigan will coordinate your travel and also monitor your progress. She's the head honcho at K19."

"That's mildly intimidating."

"I'm glad you see it that way. She's another one you won't want to disappoint."

"I won't disappoint any of you. I can promise you that," I said a second time.

"See that you keep that promise. By the way, Merrigan is in the house, talking to Esland now, if you want to head in." When Doc stood, so did I. We shook hands a second time, and I went inside.

"There she is," said Merrigan, standing.

"Am I interrupting?" I asked, looking between Doc's wife and True.

"Not at all. In fact, I have monopolized far too much of Merrigan's time as it is."

"I've enjoyed it ever so much."

"She knew my mother."

"What fun! Well?" I asked.

"Very well, in fact," answered Merrigan.

"I'll excuse myself and let the two of you talk," said True, thanking Merrigan again before she walked away.

"Please sit down," she said to me and did the same.

Merrigan briefed me on what my itinerary would be. The only thing neither of us knew was the start date. "Did Kade mention you'll also be training with Burns Butler and Leech Hess?"

My eyes widened. "He didn't."

"Burns and Leech are—what is the American expression? Old school. While Burns is a technological savant, he'll still teach you how to do your job without using it. You never know when the bad guys might find a way to hack into your systems. You need to know what to do when that happens."

"Makes sense."

"As far as Leech goes, he's the best on-the-ground operative there ever was. I'm told you already possess the Whittaker stealth. That will serve you well. More than you'll ever know, since to you, it isn't a big deal. Other agents will want you to train them, but no matter how much training they have, they'll never be as good as you are."

I didn't know what to say. I didn't consider myself particularly good at anything. I looked up at Merrigan, who was smiling.

"Darrow, tell me, can you draw?"

"Draw?"

"Yes, as in art. Pencils, paper, sketches."

"No, not at all."

"It's the same thing. Those who possess the talent have no idea how unique or special it is. To them, everyone can draw; those who say they can't, aren't trying hard enough."

It was a good analogy. "Thank you."

"I'm sure Kade has told you, you've earned this. Don't throw it away."

"I wouldn't. Never."

"I have to ask, what about Quint Alexander?" said Merrigan.

I took a deep breath and let it out slowly. "If it weren't for Quint, I wouldn't be sitting here talking with you. I can assure you, if I gave any indication that I didn't want to continue my training, he'd be the first to tell me to get back at it."

"Do you see a future with him?"

I shook my head, willing my eyes not to fill with tears. "I do not."

"Do you have any further questions for me?"

"About my training or anything?"

Merrigan smiled. "Anything within reason."

"Can you tell me about your training?"

34

Quint

I walked into the kitchen and answered a call that came in from Deck.

"What can I do for ya? Thought you were headin' out?"

"I am. Waiting to board, but I heard something I want to bring to your attention."

"What's that?"

"It's about the Palmyer place."

"What about it?" The ranch was not far from King-Alexander, but another property separated the two.

"Word is that old man Palmyer cut his two sons out of his will. Left everything to his daughter's kid."

"Cassie?"

"That's right. You know she married Cody James a while back?"

"Yep. I was at the wedding."

"As you can imagine, Mav and Bran are fit to be tied."

I'd never liked Maverick or Brandon Palmyer. Never trusted them. Evidently, their father hadn't either. "What are you thinking, Decker? It isn't something we should get involved in."

"I agree, but those kids need our support. Her uncles are gonna be doin' everything they can to see to it they fail, that is if contesting the will doesn't work."

"Understood." The ranchers in the region all stuck together. We always had. If one was in trouble, the rest would line up to help. After the storm that took so many head of cattle, we'd banded together to lick our wounds and make a plan to build our operations back up to the levels they were before the freak blizzard hit.

Knowing the young couple had to watch their backs against two of their own was a damn shame and a terrible way to start their life together. Once things got back to normal here, I'd reach out to them and let them know they could count on me for anything they needed. I'd also mention it to some of the other ranchers, although in a community like ours, news spread fast. It was likely most everyone already knew about the will and that Mav and Bran had been cut out of it.

"Thanks for filling me in," I said before ending the call with Deck. "Enjoy your trip."

"This ain't a vacation."

I knew it and wished it were. If anyone at the ranch needed one, it was Decker. The man essentially had two full-time jobs, and neither was easy.

I'd been back out on the ranch an hour when Edge told me he was going to head back in.

"What about you fellers?" I asked Ranger and Diesel. "You ready to call it a day?"

"How much daylight do we have left?" asked Ranger.

"Another hour or so."

"If you're not going in, I'll stay out with you."

"Me too," said Diesel.

"Let's head over to Schoolhouse."

We'd just ridden over a crest and dismounted when I saw two men coming toward us and four more coming from either side. Before I could so much as pull my gun, I was knocked unconscious.

35

Darrow

Merrigan had just excused herself to look for Doc when an alert popped up on my mobile.

Wellie's gone. Tell Axel, the message from Thornton read.

I clapped my hand over my mouth as a cry came up from my chest. I tried to ring my brother at the same time I ran down the hallway and pounded on the door of the bedroom where I knew Axel and True were.

"Coming," I heard him say.

"It's Wellie," I said, dissolving into sobs in Axel's arms.

"No," he said, holding me tight to him. "It can't be," he muttered.

"Where is Esland?" asked Axel, wiping his tears and turning around to look for her.

"I don't know. She was just here."

Axel walked over to the bedside table and picked up his mobile and looked at the screen.

"Who contacted you?" he asked.

"Thornton sent a text asking me to tell you about Wellie, that he'd…" I dissolved into tears. "I tried to ring him, but the call didn't go through, so I came to find you. I'm so sorry, Axel."

He looked at the screen on his mobile. "My call isn't going through either. Let me see his message."

I handed my mobile to him.

"Swipe it and then enter your code."

When I tried, first nothing happened, and then an error message came on the screen.

"Try again."

I did and got the same error message.

"Something's off. We need to find Esland."

I nodded but was too stunned to move.

"Darrow!" he shouted, shaking me. "You go find Doc or Quint, anyone at all. I'll go around back and look for Esland."

"I haven't been able to find Quint," I said when Axel came around from the back of the house.

"I haven't found Esland either."

Both Doc and Merrigan were fussing with their mobiles. "Something has jammed the signal," said Doc, pulling out his gun. He fired once, counted five seconds, and then fired again, repeating the sequence one more time. "Where the hell is Decker?"

"Out of town," I said. We waited a few moments but didn't see anyone or hear a response. "I know the property. I can head out on horseback," I offered.

"I'll go with you." Merrigan pointed to their vehicle. "Kade, you and Axel take the 4x4 and look as well."

Doc was already inside the SUV by the time Merrigan finished her sentence. He tried to start it, but it wouldn't turn on.

"There are ATVs in the barn!" I shouted, running toward it. Axel and Doc followed.

"Jesus bloody Christ!" Axel yelled, pointing to one of the stalls.

Merrigan raced over. *"It's Edge! He has a pulse. I'll stay with him; you go!"*

I had the keys to the ATVs. "This will be faster than on horseback," I said, tossing one set to Axel.

"I'll head north," he said after Doc told us he'd work on getting the security systems back up and running.

I went west, to the terrain I knew best. The Schoolhouse pasture was the highest. Maybe from there I'd be able to see where Quint and the others were. It was a long shot, and we were quickly losing daylight. What choice did we have but to look?

As I rode up the crest, three saddled horses ran past me in the opposite direction. One was Gunsmoke; I was certain of it. I gunned the ATV over the hill and saw three bodies lying on the ground.

"Quint!" I screamed, pulling out my gun and firing three shots at five-second intervals, praying that someone would hear and send help.

Quint came to while I was checking his pulse.

"What happened?"

"Ambush," he said, rubbing his head. "Check those two."

I knelt down to check the first man's pulse and saw it was Ranger. He was still alive. I was about to check the second man's, Diesel, when I heard a single gunshot.

"They're both alive," I told Quint before firing two more shots at five-second intervals in response to the single shot I'd heard. I had no way of knowing if that had been a response to me or not.

Quint sat up and tried to stand. "Fire two more, Darrow," he said, sitting back down.

I could hear the ATV approaching before I saw it. "Thank God."

"Where the hell is everybody?" Quint shouted. "We've got twenty men working this ranch. Where the fuck did they all disappear to?"

"Something is very wrong, Quint. Esland has disappeared too."

Just then, Axel came over the crest.

"We were ambushed," Quint shouted at him.

"Were you on horseback?" Axel asked as he climbed off the ATV and raced over to where I tended to Ranger and Diesel.

"Like I said, we were ambushed. Must've been ten of them at least. Might've had a chance, but we weren't on the horses at the time. Bastards must've scared 'em off after they knocked us out."

"Did you see or hear anything?"

"They were Englishmen; I can tell you that much."

I helped Ranger sit up when he came to. Quint got up, came over, and helped him to his feet. He walked him over to the ATV just as Diesel came to as well.

"What the fuck?" he groaned, trying to sit up. Axel caught him as he fell back toward the ground.

"It'll be easier for me to find my way back to you. I'll take Ranger and come back with the truck," said Quint, climbing on the ATV.

"They've been disabled," I told him.

"The Bummer sure as hell hasn't," Quint shouted as he raced off.

Diesel groaned. When he held out his hand, it was bloody. "Help is on the way," I told him and then turned to Axel. "You go. I'll wait here for Quint to come back."

"Jesus. What the hell happened?"

I repeated what Quint had said about being ambushed. He shook his head. "I don't remember a damn thing."

I looked up at the sky, then closed my eyes. "Please, God, keep True safe," I whispered. I prayed too that the text about Wellie was somehow a mistake, but how could it be?

I opened my eyes when I heard the vehicle referred to as the Bummer approaching. I was helping Diesel up when Quint and Ranger raced over to assist.

By the time we got back to the ranch, emergency vehicles had arrived. I could see Edge sitting on the bumper of one of them.

"Check these two out first," Quint shouted, pointing at Ranger and Diesel as the EMTs tried to do the same to him.

"I think I might've hit on something," said Doc, just as Axel pulled up on the ATV. He motioned him and me over to where he stood near the barn.

"Whoever hacked into the system must not have realized that the drones would continue recording even when sabotaged. They didn't shut them down completely, although they probably thought they had," he explained. "Essentially, all they did was block the signals temporarily."

"*Where is this?*" Axel shouted to Quint, who rushed over to look.

"About three miles due south." He pointed to the largest structure. "That's a cowshed; it's all open. The smaller structures are where we keep equipment. Those are enclosed buildings. Looks like they're in the shop area. We'll take the Bummer."

I climbed into the front with Quint and told the others in the back to hang on to whatever they could. "This is not a smooth ride," I warned.

Axel leaned forward and put his hand on my shoulder. "I talked to Wellie. He's fine."

"Oh, thank God," I gasped.

Axel grabbed the roll bar when Quint gunned the Bummer and went barreling in the direction of the buildings Doc had shown us.

When we were close, Quint slammed on the brakes, turned off the lights, cut the engine, and motioned in the direction each of us should go in. I got out and followed Axel. As we got closer to the building, I slowed when he did, creeping through the brush.

He motioned for me to go to the left window while he went to the right on the same side. We both listened to the men inside.

"She's no use alive," I heard one man say. "MI5 has the evidence. Even if you were able to retrieve it, it's too late. Most of it has been scanned into the system already. I need the bitch *dead.* Once she is, you'll have more money than you know what to do with to silence what few witnesses are left—by any means possible."

"What the fuck are you about?" another shouted. "You don't fucking tell us what to do. You wanna end up like this wanker? Keep running your bloody mouth, and I'll see to it you do. You didn't deliver any better than he did. 'I'm on the bloody case. I'll intercept the diaries.' Fucking useless is what you are."

"Don't forget there's close to a billion pounds on the line, which you won't get any of if you kill me."

I motioned with my head for Axel to come to where I stood.

"What was that?" one of the men said when Axel crept over.

"Settle the fuck down, Beau. Probably an animal," said the one who had been insisting they shoot True. "I told you the security systems, as well as the mobile signals, have been scrambled. They'll never bloody find us."

"I pulled the starters on all of the vehicles," said another voice.

"Make a bloody decision whether you want to kill her or keep her alive. We need to get the fuck out of here."

When I flinched, Axel turned his head toward me. "He's got her," I mouthed, raising my gun and taking aim.

"When you've got the shot, bloody take it," he whispered. I nodded and adjusted my aim while Axel crept around to the building's entrance.

Breathe. Relax. Aim. Slack. Squeeze. With the final word, I fired, and then immediately fired again. Both shots hit their target. The second, piercing the man holding True right between the eyes.

Moments later, Axel, Quint, and Doc burst through the door, firing. The rest of the men inside fell to the ground.

I raced around the back of the building, over to the other side, checking for anyone else who Quint, Doc, or Axel may have missed.

As I rounded the corner to the entrance, Axel came out with True in his arms.

"How does she seem?" I asked while we waited for Quint to bring the Bummer closer.

"I don't know yet."

"I was so bloody scared, Axel. Why did my first kill have to be in order to save the life of my best friend?"

I walked forward to open the vehicle's door. From inside, Quint took True from Axel's arms. Once he'd climbed in, Quint gently rested her on Axel's lap.

Quint climbed out and wrapped his arms around me and I dissolved into a flood of tears.

"I'm proud of you, my sweet Shadow," he murmured.

"I was so scared," I whispered.

"I know you were, but you did what needed to be done. You saved Esland's life."

Adrenaline surged through my bloodstream, my heart was pounding, sweat poured off me, and my senses were overloaded.

"Get in, sweetheart," said Quint, opening the door and helping me climb onto the front bench seat.

"They knocked her out with something; that's obvious, I know," said Doc, pulling out his phone and punching at the screen. "Merrigan says the EMTs are still at the house. They'll be able to do a more thorough job than I can now."

When I heard True's voice, I turned in the seat to look at her.

"Axel? Where am I?" she asked.

He helped her sit up. "You're safe, my love. It's all over."

True closed her eyes. "What happened? My head is bloody throbbing."

"Don't try to talk yet. We'll be at the house soon, and there are emergency personnel waiting to look you over."

"Hodges was in on it," I heard True say to Axel. "And Pique. I knew better than to trust that bloody bastard."

Axel nodded and looked up at me.

"What happened to him?" asked True.

"He's dead, sweetness," Axel told her.

"I suppose that's better."

My eyes met hers, and they filled with tears. "I killed him," I whispered.

"Thank you," True whispered back, tearing up as well.

36

Quint

Like I had most of the night, I held Darrow while she continued to sleep. When she woke, I did too. When she fell back to sleep, I let myself go with her.

I couldn't say I knew how she felt; I didn't. I'd never had to kill another human and hoped to hell I never did. Regardless of whether it was justified, it didn't matter. Darrow took a life, and that would haunt her.

I brushed her long hair away from her beautiful face, and studied her, trying my damnedest to memorize every angle, every line, the sound of her breathing—everything, because soon she'd be gone and I might never see her again.

There'd been too many times to count when I'd thought I might live out my life as a bachelor. I'd been with women I liked well enough, but not for more than a date or two. I couldn't say I'd even dated half the women I'd had sex with. That was all it had been. But this woman? She was as different as they came. She crawled straight into my heart, and that's where she'd stay. For the rest of my life, Darrow would be the one I loved and the one who got away.

I leaned down and touched my lips to hers.

"Good morning," she murmured, kissing me back. "What time is it?"

"A little after ten."

She held up the sheet. "You're naked."

I wrapped my arm around her and grabbed her ass. "As are you, darlin."

"Didn't you ride out this morning?"

"Sure didn't."

"I'm sorry."

I scratched my chin. "I'm curious what you're sorry for."

"You stayed with me instead of doing what you needed to do."

I rolled onto my back, bringing Darrow with me. "I'd be perfectly happy stayin' right here in this bed all damn day."

"But…"

I shook my head. "The hands can take care of whatever needs to be done. We've got plenty of help."

I cupped the side of her face. "Tell me how you're doing this morning, Darrow."

"I'm okay," she said, resting her body on mine so her head was right above my heart.

"Tell me what you need."

"I don't know. Nothing, really. Fundamentally, I know that I did what needed to be done."

"Very pragmatic of you."

She shrugged. "Maybe it hasn't hit me yet."

I didn't need to remind her that she'd literally fallen apart in my arms. She might not even remember having done it. As long as she knew I was here for her if she needed me, that was all I could do.

"I wonder how True is this morning."

"Probably a lot like you are. Still in shock to a certain extent."

"I should talk to her."

"This first, though." I put my fingertips on her chin and leaned down to kiss her.

Darrow shifted her weight and sat up so she was straddling my stomach. With both hands on her waist, I lifted her up and brought her down on my cock. Darrow's eyes met mine.

"This is you, baby. Take what you need," I said. "Fast, slow, deep, hard—whatever feels good, Darrow."

She rested her hands on my chest and let her body set our rhythm. I reached up and covered her breasts with my hands, alternating running the tip of my finger around the areola and pinching her nipples. She closed her eyes, threw her head back, curved her body, and quickened her pace. I watched every move she made, again trying to memorize everything I could about her.

"Quint," she groaned.

"Come on, baby, give it to me."

She opened her eyes and gazed into mine when I felt her clenching on me, and I nodded. "Come with me, Darrow."

When she fell against me, I wrapped my arms around her. I could feel her tears on my chest and tightened my grip.

"I don't want to leave," she whispered.

"I know you don't."

"But I have to."

"I know that too."

37

Darrow

I stood at the bedroom door and knocked.

"Come in," True responded.

"Am I intruding?" I asked when Axel walked toward me.

"Yes," he said at the same time True said no.

"I have some calls to make."

I walked past him over to where True sat.

"Don't leave on my account," I said after the door closed behind him.

"Are you okay?" True asked when I sat down on the bed.

"Me? I wasn't the one kidnapped."

"No, but you were the one who had to kill a man last night. I don't know how to thank you for saving my life."

"I'm okay, True. I promise."

"Merrigan told me you were struggling and that you were with Quint."

"I was with Quint." I winked. "And you know I'm not a morning person. Since he was willing to sleep in, so did I."

"I'm happy for you, Darrow."

"I appreciate that, True, but don't forget what I told you when we talked at the abbey."

True nodded.

"Plus, I'm leaving with Doc and Merrigan tomorrow."

"You are?"

"I'm training with—get this—Leech Hess and Burns Butler."

It wasn't a surprise that True had no idea who they were; I hadn't until recently. When I told her a bit about them, her eyes lit up.

"You should interview them and write a book."

True's eyes scrunched. "Wouldn't most everything be classified?"

"Maybe, but you could always make them into fictional characters."

"Good idea," she said as if she was actually mulling the idea over.

"When are you returning to England?" I asked.

"When it's safe, I suppose. I believe Axel is talking to Z now. Um…"

"What?"

"Darrow, I don't know how to thank you for what you did, but more importantly, I want you to know that I admire you more than I'd ever admired anyone."

"More than Merrigan?" I asked with another wink.

"Far more than Merrigan," True answered. "If you hadn't had the balls to follow your dreams, do you realize I'd be dead right now?"

"That isn't true…True." We both smiled. "There was a team."

She shook her head. "I'm letting you off on a humble hook. You saved my bloody life, and I don't know how to thank you."

"Be happy. That's how you can thank me. You and Axel, be happy."

My eyes filled with tears. There was so much more I wanted to say, but I couldn't utter a word of it.

Be happy because I can't. Be happy because I made the choice to follow this dream, which means I'll never have what you have.

"I want you to be happy too."

I got up and walked to the bedroom door. "Some of us can't have both, True," I said, walking out.

I saw Quint sitting at the dining table. When our eyes met, he stood and held out his hand.

"Let's go for a ride."

"I'd love that."

"Darrow, wait. We need to talk," said Axel, who I hadn't realized was also in the room.

I shook my head and kept walking. Whatever he had to say, I couldn't hear right now. It wasn't that I was jealous of True and Axel as much as I was jealous that they were walking into a new life that they would share together while tomorrow I'd be walking away alone.

"They're leaving," Quint said once we were in the barn.

"Okay."

He came over and cupped my cheek. "And so are you."

I took a step back, and Quint dropped his hand.

"Just for tonight, could we pretend I'm not leaving?"

"Sure we can. Tell me what you want to do."

"I want to ride, and then I want to go to the Branch and eat a massive T-bone, and then I want to dance until I can't stand having your body grind against mine without both of us being naked, and then I want to come back here and have sex until I can't walk."

"I think I can handle all of that."

"You're the only man I know who can, Quint."

"Let's do this, Shadow. Let's have a night that neither of us will ever forget."

I studied the man who held my heart, the man I loved like I'd never loved anyone, and the man who, after tomorrow, I may never see again. If he was willing to make this a night we'd never forget, so was I.

"I thought we were sleeping in," I groaned the next morning when I opened my eyes and saw Quint was awake. I put my forearm over my face to block out the sun. Quint leaned down and laved my nipple.

"God, Quint," I groaned, holding his head to my breast.

"Are you sore, baby?" he asked, moving one hand lower until it rested on my pussy.

I shook my head.

"Not good enough. Let me hear the words."

I pushed him onto his back, nipped at his neck, and trailed my lips down his body.

"Shadow," he scolded.

"I'm leaving today, Quint. If I'm sore, I'll recover."

"Come here." He pulled me up the front of his body so my chin rested on his sternum. "Let's shower."

"Showering means getting out of bed."

He rolled so I was under him, then stood. "You have an early flight out."

"I do, which is why I don't want to waste time now."

"I like the idea of leaving you wanting more," he said, walking naked from the bed into the bathroom.

I didn't follow. I couldn't. If I showered with him, it would be the last time I did. If we made love, it would be the last time we did that too. Even waking up in each other's arms—that was for the last time. I rolled over and put the pillow over my head, wishing for the millionth time that Quint would ask me to stay here with him. I knew he wouldn't, but that didn't stop me from wishing it.

Why had I agreed to leave with Doc and Merrigan today? Because if I hadn't, I'd be flying back to England rather than just out to California. At least, by continuing my training on the Central Coast, there was a possibility Quint might come to visit.

He came out of the bathroom and put on a pair of jeans, but didn't button the fly all the way.

"Are you sure there isn't anything I can do for you, cowboy?"

"You know I can't get enough of you, Shadow," he groaned, letting his jeans slide back down. "Like what you see, darlin'?" he teased when I licked my lips.

Quint kissed the back of my hand and slid in beside me. He put his arm around me, and I rested my head on his chest.

"This is a great opportunity for you, Shadow. I remember hearing stories about Burns Butler and Leech Hess from my pa."

"Yes. Quite the opportunity."

"Go out and grab your dreams, Shadow. Don't tell me to ask you to stay."

"I don't know when I'll ever be back." My eyes filled with tears.

"So be it, darlin'."

"That's it? What will be, will be? What if we never see one another again?"

"Like I said, Darrow. So be it."

I rolled away from him. "I thought I mattered to you."

Before I realized what was happening, I was on my back and Quint was on top of me.

"You do matter to me."

When I tried to look away, Quint put his fingertips on my chin and turned my head so we were face-to-face. He kissed me so hard and so deeply that it hurt. I felt his cock against me. With one thrust, he buried himself in my pussy, pounding into me. Instead of pushing, he slowed his movement and stopped. He stared at me so intently, I wanted to turn my head again, but didn't. My eyes met his, and I waited.

"Letting you go is the hardest thing I've ever done, but I don't have a choice. You have to follow your dreams, Darrow."

"Leaving you is the hardest thing I've ever done."

When Quint went out to the barn, I told him I'd be right behind him. Instead, I went looking for Merrigan, whom I found sitting at the dining room table.

"Can we chat for a minute?" I asked.

"Of course." Merrigan motioned for me to take a seat.

"I'd rather do it somewhere we won't be interrupted."

"Very well," said Merrigan, following me to the front porch.

"There is no easy way to say this, and I want you to know how much I appreciate everything you and Doc offered me, but I can't accept it. I'm returning to the UK."

"I see. When did this come about?"

"Just now."

Merrigan's eyes scrunched as she studied me. "I don't see this as a wise decision on your part, but it is your life."

"I appreciate you respecting my decision."

"Certainly, and, Darrow, if you ever change your mind, the offer to train with K19 will remain open."

My heart ached, not just with Merrigan's evident disappointment in me, but with my realization that Quint was, in fact, letting me go. It didn't matter that I'd be training in the States; when I told him I was afraid I'd never return to the ranch, he'd been nonchalant in his response.

"So be it," he'd said. He had admitted he cared about me, but nothing more. The last words he'd said only reiterated that he had no choice but to let me go.

I stood and walked back into the house, picked up my mobile, and searched for flights leaving later that morning. There was one I could make if I left within the hour.

38

Quint

I was too stunned to speak; I just stared at Darrow.

"It's for the best," she said.

"You're really going back to England?"

"That's right. My dream was always to be an MI6 agent, to work for Her Majesty, not for a private company in the States."

"I see."

"I appreciate everything you've done for me, Quint. If it hadn't been for you, I wouldn't be doing this at all."

"Sure you would be," I said, shaking my head.

"I need to go if I'm going to catch my flight."

"I can take you to the airport."

"Doc and Merrigan offered their rental." She stepped forward and put her arms around me. "It's better this way. Goodbye, Quint."

"Goodbye, Darrow." I kissed the top of her head, let her go, and watched as she walked out of my life—this time for good.

39

Darrow

I'd only been on the road for ten minutes when I passed by two vehicles on the shoulder. It looked as though an argument between two men and a couple was taking place. I slowed the 4x4 to get a better look and saw the young woman was obviously crying.

I hadn't gotten much farther when I looked back and saw the two men grab the couple and force them toward another vehicle. I spun the SUV around, but by the time I got back to where I saw the argument taking place, the vehicle I'd seen the couple forced into had gone off the road and was barreling across a field. I followed.

They drove to an isolated pasture and I stayed on them, wishing I was in the Bummer rather than a regular 4x4.

When the truck stopped near an outbuilding, one of the men jumped out and started firing in my direction, hitting one of the tires, causing the 4x4 to come to a stop on the rugged terrain. I jumped out, my gun at the ready and prepared to fire back, using the vehicle's door as a shield.

I took a deep breath, relaxed my shoulders, took aim even though I was under fire myself, slacked, and squeezed. Like I had with Pique, I hit the man right between the eyes, and he fell to the ground.

In those split seconds, I saw that the second man had dragged the two other people into the outbuilding. I ran toward the rear, knowing I had little to no coverage if the man started firing at me from the inside.

I was almost to the other side when I saw him come out the front at the same moment I smelled smoke.

"Bugger me," I shouted, kicking in the back door of the building as flames engulfed the front. The couple were both bound and gagged, but I didn't have time to untie them. If I tried, we'd all be overcome by smoke, if not flames. If I could get them out of the structure, it might buy me enough time to untie them before the fire spread to where we were.

I grabbed the back of the woman's shirt and pulled her the short distance to the door and then went back inside to do the same with the man. I was just about to untie them when I saw the other man light the grass near the 4x4. When he saw me, he drew his gun, but I was quicker. I broke the shot and hit the man in the chest. He got off one more shot before the truck exploded into a ball of flames.

"We need to get out of here quickly!" I yelled, untying the man first so he could help free the woman.

"You've been shot," he said once the gag was out of his mouth. I looked down and saw my blouse was soaked with blood. It was the last thing I remembered.

40

Quint

"There's a wildfire on Palmyer!" Decker yelled as he came flying in the kitchen door.

I turned the heat off on the stove where I'd been cooking breakfast.

"What are you doing back?"

"That isn't important right now. Did you not hear me? There's a wildfire on Palmyer!"

"How bad?"

"Four-alarm. I'm heading there now." I followed Deck out of the kitchen, wiping my hands and pulling on my boots.

Merrigan and Doc came running in. "I heard someone say there's a fire," she said.

"If it's four-alarm, it's bad."

"I'll come with you," said Doc.

"You have a flight—"

"We own the fucking plane, Quint. Let's go!" Doc yelled, pushing me out the front door.

"Wait!" yelled Merrigan. *"I'm coming with you."*

"I need you to stay here and alert the crew," I yelled back. "If it's that bad, we need to start cutting fire lines. Tell anyone you can find to bring the backhoes and alert the other ranchers."

"Where is Palmyer?" asked Doc.

"It isn't one of ours," I said, motioning for him to follow. "We'll take the Bummer. It can get through almost anything." I pulled one of the barn's alley doors open, and Doc and I climbed in.

"How far away are we?" Doc asked.

"About ten miles as the crow flies, which is the way we're gonna go. It's owned by a young couple who inherited from her grandpa."

My jaw was tight as my mind raced, wondering if Cassie's uncles had anything to do with the fire starting. I prayed not, because if they had, there'd be a slew of ranchers ready to beat them into the ground. "Can you grab that and turn it up?" I said to Doc, motioning with my head to the handheld radio.

When he did, we could hear Deck's voice. "It's bad. The cattle are surrounded."

When the radio cut out, I pulled off the main road. We crested a ridge and took in the scene in front of us.

There was no question that the fire had engulfed the herd and was burning out of control.

"Pray for those kids," I said quietly, turning the vehicle back toward the road. The way I'd originally been headed was directly in the fire's path.

"Is King-Alexander in danger?" Doc asked.

"Not at the moment, but with the way the wind is kicking up, there isn't a stretch of land that isn't at risk."

I drove up to a line of trucks. The smoke was too thick for us to see very far. Doc and I jumped out and ran over to where Decker stood with several other men. As we approached, I saw their hats were off and many were wiping their faces and covering their mouths with bandannas like I was.

Before I could ask Decker what the status of the fire was, there was a loud roar; a tanker flew over and made a retardant drop on the flames. A moment later, two smaller planes flew over and dropped water. My eyes burned, and it was impossible to see anything through the thick smoke.

"What's happening?" I yelled.

"The fire chief said to wait here. He'll be right over to talk to us. We need to get the backhoes here."

"Already on their way," I yelled in response.

"I heard someone else say somethin' about draftin' from the water tanks," Deck shouted.

Both things we could do to help.

"Any word on Cody and Cass?" I asked.

I was close enough to see Deck shake his head. I didn't like the look I saw in his eyes.

"Fuck. I'll kill those bastards with my bare hands if those kids are hurt and Cassie's uncles had anything to do with this."

As loud as it was, I didn't think anyone had heard me, but I knew Deck had when I heard him say he'd be right there with me.

"Quint!" yelled John "Mac" MacIver, the sheriff as well as chief of the volunteer fire company the ranchers set up to help with the county units. He was also a man I'd known all my life. He approached and motioned for us to follow him back farther away from the line of trucks.

"What can we do, Mac?" I asked.

"I need you to set up a command center for the ranchers that want to help. I need them to get about a mile back."

"Done," I said. "What else?"

"I need men to get in front of this thing and start cutting fire lines." Mac looked at Deck. "You know this place as well as anybody else. You get with Brownie and figure out where the natural lines are." Mac turned back to me. "Once he's done that, you start sending guys out. Who's that?" Mac asked, pointing to Doc.

"Doc Butler."

"He's a big *sonuvabitch*. Got any law enforcement experience?"

"Special forces good enough?"

"Hell, yeah," said Mac, motioning for Doc to join us.

"You're the new sheriff in town," Mac said to him. "I need you to get these men out of our way. Quint is gonna set up a command center a mile that way." Mac pointed behind us. "I don't want to see a single civilian on this side of it unless they're in a backhoe ready to cut lines."

"How big do the lines need to be?" I asked.

"Big. Ten to twenty feet wide with a three- to four-foot scrape," Mac answered.

"What about water tank draws?" asked Decker.

"Get someone from each ranch on it."

"Wait," said Decker when Mac started to walk away. "What about Cody and Cass?"

Mac shook his head. "We found two bodies, Deck. The wind must've shifted. They haven't been identified, but chances are good it's them."

"*Fuck!*" Deck shouted, looking away. "*Jesus fucking Christ,*" he cried.

Mac put his hand on Decker's shoulder. "I need you to get it together, son. I need your help. *They* need your help."

"I'm together," Deck told Mac and then looked at me. "If I find out this was set intentionally, you'll be seein' me in prison."

"I'll be right there with you."

Forty-eight hours after the call had come in about the Palmyer fire, Deck and I were on our way back to King-Alexander Ranch. When I'd insisted Deck take a break to get some rest, the man said the only way he'd leave was if I did too.

I pulled up to the house, climbed out of the Bummer, and walked over to the barn. I peeled the sooty, wet clothes from my body and threw them into the waste pile. I grabbed some other clothes from the tack room, pulled on my spare pair of work boots, not bothering to lace them up, and walked over to the house.

It was daylight, but otherwise, I had no idea what time it was. As soon as I showered, I planned to fall into bed and sleep until my body woke on its own.

When that happened, it was dark. I got up, looked out the window, and then back at the empty bed. I knew it made me a selfish asshole, but more than anything, I wished Darrow was asleep in it.

Every hour I'd spent in the backhoe, cutting the lines, I thought about her. I also thought about Cody and Cassie. They were two kids, crazy in love, starting their life together. That they were gone was a tragedy too hard to bear.

I got back in bed, buried my head in a pillow, and let the tears I'd fought so hard against, flow.

I'd cried two other times in my life that I remembered. The first was when my mother died. The second was the night I'd come into the house alone after the blizzard, wishing so much I could've done something more to save my herd. I remembered wishing Darrow was there to comfort me that night, just like I wished she was now. Somehow, I fell back to sleep.

"Quint. Sorry I woke you," my father said when I found my phone and answered the incoming call.

"It's okay," I responded, my voice thick with sleep.

"It's about Darrow."

I sat up. "What about her?"

"She wasn't on the flight, and I haven't been able to reach her or anyone else. What's going on?"

I told Z about the fire and how we'd all been working around the clock. "Darrow left before it started. She was on her way to the airport."

"You're certain?"

"Absolutely."

"I don't like this. I know Darrow has disappeared before, but when I talked to her about her desire to decline the offer from K19 and return to MI6, she seemed determined."

"I'll talk to Merrigan and see if she's heard from her."

I ended the call and got out of bed. I still had no idea what time it was, but at least it was daylight. After throwing on some clothes, I went to the kitchen. I saw Merrigan on the front porch, on her phone. Maybe Z had decided to check with her himself.

"Quint," she said, coming back inside. "I didn't know you were here."

"I came back sometime yesterday but went straight to bed."

"As did Kade. Listen, I just got off the phone with—"

"Z? I already talked to him."

"No, actually, with the rental car company. They said the 4x4 hasn't been returned."

I gripped the cabinet to steady myself. "Fuck," I muttered.

"What?" gasped Merrigan.

"Z said that Darrow wasn't on her flight."

"Dear God," she said. "Where is she?"

41

Darrow

I opened my eyes and looked around, trying to figure out where I was. It appeared I was in the hospital. Several machines were humming around me, and I had an IV in my arm. I raised my head when someone came in.

"Look who's awake," the woman said, walking over to me. "How do you feel?"

"Feel? I've no idea. Why am I here?"

"You lost a great deal of blood. In fact, if they hadn't gotten you here so quickly, you might not have made it. Fortunately, they did, and we were able to get you straight into surgery."

"Who got me here?"

"Cody and Cassie James, but I have a more important question for you. Can you tell me your name? You came in with no identification whatsoever."

"Darrow," I said, bringing my hand to my throbbing temple. "Whittaker. I'm Darrow Whittaker."

"What is the last thing you remember, Ms. Whittaker?"

"Fire. And an explosion. There were two people. A man and a woman."

"Cody and Cassie, as I said. You saved their lives by pulling them away from the fire."

I winced when I tried to sit up straighter.

"Let me raise the bed," said the woman. "You're still recovering from surgery."

"Why did I have surgery?"

"You had a bullet lodged not far from your heart, Ms. Whittaker. Don't you remember being shot?"

I shook my head. "What day is it?"

"Friday."

"I was supposed to leave two days ago."

"Where were you going?" the woman asked while she checked the various machines and their attachments to my body.

"Back to England."

"My guess is there are people who are quite worried about you. The doctor is on his way here now. After he's finished examining you, we'll see if we can contact your family."

I closed my eyes and rested my head against the pillow.

"She's awake," I heard another woman's voice say.

I opened my eyes and saw the woman's were filled with tears. "Hi. Are you Cassie?"

"I am. Thank God you're okay."

"I understand you saved my life."

When a man came around to stand behind her, I asked if he was Cody.

"I am, ma'am, but we didn't save your life. You saved ours."

"What's your name?" Cassie asked.

"Darrow Whittaker. I was a guest at King-Alexander Ranch. They're probably quite concerned about me."

Cody had his mobile out and was placing a call when the nurse came back in.

"No cell phones in the ICU," she scolded and then looked at Cassie. "The doctor is here. You'll need to step out for a few minutes."

Cassie leaned over and kissed my cheek. "I won't be far," she said.

"Those two kids have been here almost every minute," said the nurse at the same time the doctor walked in. "They were so worried about you."

"I'm Dr. Wheeler," the doctor said, holding out his hand to shake mine.

"You're English."

"That I am, as are you. Although we didn't know that until now."

42

Quint

I was about to start calling area hospitals when my cell phone rang; I didn't recognize the number.

"Quint Alexander," I answered.

"Mr. Alexander, it's Cody James."

I felt the air leave my lungs and reached for the kitchen counter. "Is this a joke? Whoever this is, I don't—"

"I'm sorry to interrupt you, sir. I guess you haven't heard. The bodies they found weren't Cassie's and mine, but what I'm calling about is more important. Do you know someone by the name of Darrow Whittaker?"

"Darrow? Yes. Where is she?"

"She's at St. Joseph's in the ICU. We didn't know who she was until now."

I had a thousand questions, but they could wait. "I'm on my way."

"Who was that?" asked Merrigan.

"Cody James. He said that Darrow is at St. Joseph's hospital."

"Cody James?" asked Doc, walking over.

"That's right. I don't understand what's going on myself, but all that matters is getting to Darrow."

"We'll come with you," said Merrigan.

The hospital was twenty minutes away, but the drive there had never felt longer. The entire time, Merrigan was on the phone, trying to find out more about Darrow's condition, but since she wasn't next of kin, they wouldn't tell her anything.

"Call Shiv," Doc told her while she sat on hold.

"I wanted to know more before I called him, but I guess there's no choice."

I listened as Merrigan told Darrow's older brother the limited amount of information we knew.

"He's going to ring the duchess now and ask her to contact the hospital, given she's Darrow's legal next of kin," Merrigan said, ending the call just as I pulled into the hospital parking lot.

"Pull up to the front," said Doc. "I'll park it."

"Thanks." I jumped out of the truck and Merrigan followed me straight into the elevator. The doors opened directly to the ICU check-in desk on the fourth floor.

"I'm Quint Alexander, here to see Darrow Whittaker," I said to the woman sitting there.

"She's in room 412, but only relatives are allowed into the ICU. Are you related to Ms. Whittaker?"

"I'm her husband," I barked.

"Please sign here, and then you can go in. Who is this with you?"

"Her sister."

The woman motioned for Merrigan to sign in as well. "It's the third room on the left," she said, buzzing us in.

"Go ahead," Merrigan said when we reached the door. "I'll wait out here."

I hadn't stopped praying since I ended the call with Cody James. I had no idea what Darrow's condition was, but that she was in the ICU meant it might be bad. I took a deep breath and opened the door.

"Thank God," I said when I saw her sitting up in bed, not looking much worse than she had the last time I saw her. I raced over and took her hand.

"Hi," she said, looking into my eyes.

"Hi." I had so many questions, the same ones I'd had when I ended the call with Cody James, but none of them mattered now any more than they had then. I leaned down and kissed her. She was the one to push her tongue into my mouth. I wanted to take her in my arms, but I had no idea how she'd been hurt. I ended our kiss and sat in the chair beside her. "How are you feeling?"

"Okay. Sore, my head is pounding, and I have no idea what happened except that I was shot and lost a lot of blood. My memory is coming back little by little, but I haven't remembered enough to piece it all together."

I didn't hear anything beyond her saying she was shot. "You don't know who shot you?"

"Only from what Cassie has told me."

"Who did she say it was?"

"Her uncle."

"Do you know what happened to him?"

Darrow's eyes scrunched, and she nodded. "I shot him. I shot the other one too." She closed her eyes and rested her head against the pillow. "There was a fire," she said, opening her eyes.

"There was. A bad one."

"One of them started it. I had to get the couple out of the shack."

I stroked her forehead. "Don't force it, sweetheart. It'll come to you." I scrubbed my face with my hand. "I want to take you in my arms and hold you close to me, but I don't want to hurt you. Do you know where you were shot?"

She pointed to a place right below her breast. "Here."

I was damn glad I was sitting down, or I might've passed out. She was shot in the chest yet she was still alive?

"Hello," a nurse said when she walked in. "I understand you're Ms. Whittaker's husband?"

"That's right." I winked at Darrow.

"Were you aware you had a husband?" the nurse asked, winking too.

Darrow smiled but didn't answer.

"Your sister is waiting in the hall. My guess is you didn't know you had one of those either." The nurse turned to me.

"If you're about to tell me to leave, you're gonna have to call security to get me outta here, and I'm not gonna make it easy on them."

The nurse rested her hand on my arm. "I was going to tell you that you can invite Ms. Whittaker's sister into the room. She's permitted two visitors at a time."

"In a minute. I need more time alone with my wife."

The nurse left after recording some things on her computer.

"Your wife? Is that right?"

I took both of Darrow's hands in mine. "If you'll have me, I'd love to be your husband."

"Quint, you don't have to—"

"What don't I have to do? Tell you how much I love you? Because I do. With all my heart."

Darrow studied me.

I reached out and cupped her cheek. "I have more to say."

"Okay," she murmured, meeting my gaze.

I cleared my throat. "If I've learned anything in the last three days, it's that life can change on a dime. As I sat in a backhoe, moving dirt, one thought kept running through my mind. I want you in my life, Darrow. Whatever it takes to make that happen, I'm willing to do. I love the ranch—it's part of who I am—but without you, I don't know that I'd love it as much. In fact, I fear I'd grow to hate it."

"What are you saying?"

"That at the end of my life, I don't want to look back and regret choosing my job over you."

"It's more than your job, Quint. You just said that the ranch is part of who you are. I could never ask—"

"You aren't asking. I'm the one asking. Or at least I'm trying to." I leaned forward and kissed her. "I love you, Darrow, and while this isn't the most romantic proposal in the world, I have to do it. Here and now. Will you marry me?"

The seconds it took her to answer, felt like hours.

"Of course I'll marry you. I love you, Quint."

I bent down and rested my head on our clasped hands. "I almost lost you," I cried, feeling the tears flow from my eyes and onto our hands. "I would've died if you had. I love you so much."

"You must understand that I won't let you leave the ranch, Quint."

"I will if that's what it takes for us to be together."

"I have another idea," said Merrigan, standing just inside the open door. "Let's reopen the discussion about you training with K19."

Darrow smiled.

"There's been a change, however, that I should make you aware of."

"What's that?" Darrow asked with wide eyes.

"You'll be training with me."

"With you?"

"That's right, with me. You're good, Darrow, and with me mentoring you, you are going to make the best bloody K19 team member there's ever been."

"No pressure or anything," said Darrow, holding her side when she laughed.

Merrigan turned to me. "We can work it out so Darrow's home base is at the ranch, just like Z's was at one time. But I beg you, Quint. Don't ask her to walk away from her training or her career."

"Never," I said, staring into my Shadow's eyes. "I love her far too much to let her walk away from her dream."

Epilogue

Darrow

July

"You're beautiful," said Quint when I came down the stairs of Bristol House, followed by Merrigan and True.

"Aren't you supposed to be with Axel?" I whispered.

"Yeah, but I had to do this first."

Quint pulled me to him and kissed me.

"You're wearing more lipstick than I am now," I teased.

Quint took a handkerchief out of his pocket and wiped his mouth. "The only reason I'm doing this is because there are going to be photos. I don't want our kids ever looking at Axel and Esland's wedding album and asking why their daddy had lipstick on."

"I love you, Mr. Alexander."

"I love you more, Mrs. Alexander."

Quint rushed off to join Axel where he stood by the garden gate, waiting to marry my best friend.

"I can't believe you two got married before we did," said True.

"I can't believe Quint insisted you do it before you left the hospital," added Merrigan.

True had asked me the night before if I regretted not having a formal wedding.

"Everything was as it was meant to be," I'd answered. "Just like you and Axel are meant to be."

Merrigan took a step forward when we heard the music begin to play.

"I'm so happy for you, True," I whispered while we waited for Merrigan to reach the gate.

"I'm so happy for you, Darrow."

I rubbed my belly as I took a step forward. "Later today, we'll tell your daddy that you're on your way," I whispered. "And after you're born, I'll tell you the story of how he almost wore lipstick to your Aunt True and Uncle Axel's wedding."

1

Decker

As I drove home from the airport after my flight back from London, something on the side of the road caught my eye. What the hell was that? Couldn't be a deer, not in these parts. It wasn't big enough to be a cow, unless it was a damn skinny one.

I stopped the truck and climbed out, at first thinking it might be a mannequin someone had tossed by the road, until it started to moan.

"What in the—" I rushed over and saw it was a woman. It was dark, and she was on her side, but I didn't recognize her. She was pretty enough that if she was from around here, I sure as hell would've.

"Don't move," I said when the woman tried to sit up. I leaned down farther and eased my hand under her head. "Can you tell me what happened?"

"I have to go," she cried, trying again to move. "He'll kill me."

"Who's gonna kill you?"

"My…"

About the Author

USA Today and Amazon Top 15 Bestselling Author Heather Slade writes shamelessly sexy, edge-of-your seat romantic suspense.

She gave herself the gift of writing a book for her own birthday one year. Forty-plus books later (and counting), she's having the time of her life.

The women Slade writes are self-confident, strong, with wills of their own, and hearts as big as the Colorado sky. The men are sublimely sexy, seductive alphas who rise to the challenge of capturing the sweet soul of a woman whose heart they'll hold in the palm of their hand forever. Add in a couple of neck-snapping twists and turns, a page-turning mystery, and a swoon-worthy HEA, and you'll be holding one of her books in your hands.

She loves to hear from my readers. You can contact her at heather@heatherslade.com

To keep up with her latest news and releases, please visit her website at www.heatherslade.com to sign up for her newsletter.

MORE FROM AUTHOR HEATHER SLADE

BUTLER RANCH

Kade's Worth

Brodie's Promise

Maddox's Truce

Naughton's Secret

Mercer's Vow

Kade's Return

Butler Ranch Christmas

WICKED WINEMAKERS
FIRST LABEL

Brix's Bid

Ridge's Release

Coming soon:

Press's Passion

Zin's Sins

K19 SECURITY
SOLUTIONS TEAM ONE

Razor's Edge

Gunner's Redemption

Mistletoe's Magic

Mantis' Desire

Dutch's Salvation

K19 SECURITY
SOLUTIONS TEAM TWO

Striker's Choice

Monk's Fire

Halo's Oath

Tackle's Honor

Onyx's Awakening

K19 SHADOW
OPERATIONS TEAM ONE

Code Name: Ranger

Code Name: Diesel

Code Name: Wasp

Code Name: Cowboy

Coming soon:

Code Name: Mayhem

THE INVINCIBLES
TEAM ONE

Decked

Undercover Agent

Edged

Grinded

Riled

Handled

Smoked

THE INVINCIBLES
TEAM TWO

Bucked

Irished

Sainted

Hammered

Ripped

THE UNSTOPPABLES
TEAM ONE

Furied

Coming soon:

Merried

Vexed

Inked

Raged

Jagged

THE ROYAL AGENTS
OF MI6

*The Duke and the
Assassin*

The Lord and the Spy

*The Commoner and
the Correspondent*

*The Rancher and
the Lady*

COWBOYS OF
CRESTED BUTTE

A Cowboy Falls

A Cowboy's Dance

A Cowboy's Kiss

A Cowboy Stays

A Cowboy Wins